"Get out!" she snapped

Jamie started to tremble, all her anger and pain welling up inside her. "You might have forced me into this marriage, Jake, but you'll never force me into your bed!"

"Come on, Jamie," Jake demanded softly. "You're a woman now...what makes you think I'll need to use force?" With a mocking gesture, he turned toward the door.

Long, long after he had gone Jamie lay tense and awake, telling herself that she would never, never submit to physically becoming Jake's wife. And yet she knew, even as she made the bitter claim, that she had already given him her heart. Even after six years he still held it—and he always would.

PENNY JORDAN was constantly in trouble in school because of her inability to stop daydreaming— especially during French lessons. In her teens she was an avid romance reader, although it didn't occur to her to try writing one herself until she was older. "My first half-dozen attempts ended up ingloriously," she remembers, "but I persevered, and one manuscript was finished." She plucked up the courage to send it to a publisher, convinced her book would be rejected. It wasn't, and the rest is history! Penny is married and lives in Cheshire.

Books by Penny Jordan

HARLEQUIN PRESENTS

850—EXORCISM
868—PERMISSION TO LOVE
883—INJURED INNOCENT
897—THE HARD MAN
916—FIRE WITH FIRE
931—CAPABLE OF FEELING
946—DESIRE NEVER CHANGES
962—A MAN POSSESSED
978—DESIRE FOR REVENGE
994—RESEARCH INTO MARRIAGE
1000—PASSIONATE RELATIONSHIP
1023—TOO SHORT A BLESSING

HARLEQUIN SIGNATURE EDITION

LOVE'S CHOICES
STRONGER THAN YEARNING

Don't miss any of our special offers. Write to us at the following address for information on our newest releases.

Harlequin Reader Service
901 Fuhrmann Blvd., P.O. Box 1397, Buffalo, NY 14240
Canadian address: P.O. Box 603,
Fort Erie, Ont. L2A 5X3

PENNY JORDAN

JORDAN

a reason for marriage

Harlequin Books

TORONTO • NEW YORK • LONDON
AMSTERDAM • PARIS • SYDNEY • HAMBURG
STOCKHOLM • ATHENS • TOKYO • MILAN

Harlequin Presents first edition January 1988
ISBN 0-373-11041-3

Original hardcover edition published in 1986
by Mills & Boon Limited

CHAPTER ONE

'JAMIE, it's great to have you here. We were so pleased that you could come. I hardly ever get to see you these days. You're looking tired though, Uncle Mark says you work very hard.'

A brief smile curled Jamie's lip-glossed mouth as her cousin mentioned her stepfather. She had been lucky there, she acknowledged mentally; more than lucky when she listened to other people's stories of their parents' second marriages.

Of course the fact that her own father had died before she was two probably had something to do with the fact that she had accepted Mark so readily; that and the fact that he had been as ready to love her as his daughter as she had him as her father.

'He exaggerates, Beth,' Jamie told her cousin, lifting her eyes from the second coat of lacquer she was applying to her nails.

Her cousin's invitation to spend the weekend with her and her husband in their Bristol home had coincided with a gap in her work schedules. But now that she was here... She stifled the sense of unease that had been growing in her ever since her arrival just after lunch.

'Tell me about my goddaughter,' she instructed her cousin. 'It's been almost six months since I last saw her.'

'And whose fault is that?' Beth challenged indignantly. '*We* went to Queensmeade for Christmas. Why weren't you there, Jamie? Your mother was bitterly disappointed.'

Guilt momentarily chased the warning coolness from her eyes as Jamie raised her head to look at her cousin.

'Business, I'm afraid. I had hoped to be there, but I was offered a contract in New York I just couldn't pass up.'

Listening to the sound of her own voice, distant and faintly aloof, Jamie had a momentary desire to break into hysterical laughter at the falsity of the image she was deliberately projecting, but she had hidden behind it for so long now that it was almost part of her.

There wasn't one member of the family now who didn't look at her and see the successful polished businesswoman she had made herself become. Glancing down at her long lacquered nails, she checked a faint sigh as she looked back to the tomboy she had once been, running wild in the large grounds of Queensmeade. But it was over ten years now since she had been that girl, and between her and the woman she now was there was a chasm that nothing could bridge—and that was the way she wanted it.

'You can become re-acquainted with my daughter tomorrow,' Beth told her firmly, refusing to be sidetracked. 'I want to hear about you. Uncle Mark is terribly proud of you, Jamie; more proud than he is of Jake, I sometimes think. I read that article about you in *Homes and Gardens* the other week, the photographs of the rooms you'd done were fantastic.'

The feature in question had been a good one and had resulted in a small avalanche of extra business for her small decorating business, Jamie reflected.

The old paint finishes and manner of decorating were becoming more and more popular, and she had never been sorry that she had decided to switch from the more traditional interior-designer career she had planned for herself to what she considered the exciting challenge of learning and improving on the traditional techniques of marbling, graining, dragging and all the other styles of paint decor which were now so fashionable.

'Whilst you're here I think I shall have to pick your brains about this place,' Beth continued wryly. 'We were full of plans when we moved in, but Richard's been so busy that we haven't been able to do so much as buy a roll of wallpaper.'

Richard, Beth's solidly placid husband, had recently decided to break from his company and set up in business on his own, and knowing the problems that could be involved Jamie could well understand that decorating would be the last item on his list of priorities.

'We'll go through the house together tomorrow,' she promised her cousin, smiling when she saw her pleased expression.

'I envy you,' the younger girl said with a faint sigh. 'You always look so glamorous.'

Shrugging fine-boned shoulders Jamie told her carelessly, 'It's just a façade, Beth, that's all; a necessary part of my business to project a glossy, expensive image, but I haven't changed, you know.'

Lifting blue eyes to her cousin's darker, almost violet ones, Beth said seriously,

'No, I know you haven't, Jamie. It's a long time since you've been to Queensmeade, isn't it?'

Catching the faint note of censure in her cousin's voice, Jamie carefully blanked out every emotion from her voice.

'The Yorkshire Dales are a long way from London.' She saw the faint flicker of something in Beth's eyes, and suddenly alarm clutched her heart-muscles. 'What is it, Beth?' she demanded huskily. 'Is something wrong at home? My mother, Mark?'

When had she started calling her stepfather Mark? To strangers it might seem that she used his Christian name to hold him at a distance, to differentiate between her stepfather and her natural father, but that wasn't the case. She had picked the habit up from Jake of course, probably almost before she realised what she was doing.

Jake had been her god in those days; a magnificent and awe-inspiring creature whom she was privileged to call 'brother'... her mouth twisted a little bitterly. It seemed incredible that she had ever been that naïve.

'I shouldn't have said anything,' Beth told her guiltily. 'It's Mark, Jamie. He's been suffering from chest pains for some time and the doctor's diagnosed a heart condition—at the moment it's not too serious, but he's been told he has to take things more easily—not to worry so much. Your mother's persuading him to retire, to hand control of the company over completely to Jake.'

It was no use pretending that it did not hurt to receive this information second-hand from her cousin, but she had no one to blame for that pain other than herself. She was, after all, the one who had deliberately distanced herself from her home, who had intentionally set out to carve herself a career that would take her as far away as possible. But she rang home regularly to speak to her mother.

'Your mother didn't want to worry you,' Beth told her sympathetically, seeing the pain in her eyes. 'She knows how close you are to Uncle Mark.'

'Umm. I don't know how on earth she's going to get him to slow down.'

Beth's expression lightened. 'Jake said exactly the same thing. Funny how the two of you invariably come up with the same reactions at the same time, and yet put you together and you can't agree on a single thing. I remember at our wedding, I thought you were about to come to blows.'

Jamie looked away from her, studying her nails thoughtfully before reaching for the lacquer bottle to apply a final coat.

'Yes,' she said carefully, her attention all for her nails, 'It's always been like that.'

'No, it hasn't.'

Her heart lurched at the quiet challenge in Beth's voice.

'Why *don't* the two of you get on any more, Jamie?' Beth pressed. 'It hurts your mother and Uncle Mark dreadfully. They both love both of you so much. Whenever there's a family gathering it's noticeable that either you or Jake will be there—but never both of you. It's almost as though it's pre-planned.'

'Well, it isn't,' Jamie told her harshly, apologising with a wry smile when she saw her cousin's faintly hurt expression. 'I'm sorry. I'm a bit on edge. I hate flying, especially across the Atlantic. I think I'm still suffering from jet-lag.'

Jet-lag? Anguish and humiliation was closer to the mark but those emotions belonged to a Jamie long dead and buried, whom she was not going to disinter for anyone.

Observing the silken gleam of her cousin's straight fall of dark red hair as she bent over her nails, Beth tactfully changed the subject, asking enviously, 'How on earth do you get your nail-polish like that?'

'It isn't hard. It just takes a good eye and a practised hand,' Jamie told her, grinning as she deftly applied the last stroke and studied the finished effect. 'Besides, who's going to employ me as a decorator if they see I can't even paint my nails?'

'But I can't even get mine that long, never mind anything else.'

'Ah well, you know what a sybaritic life I lead,' Jamie mocked, lifting one eyebrow slightly.

It wasn't fair that one person should be given so much, Beth thought, sighing for the waste of all her cousin's feminine attributes on someone who declared openly and coolly that she had no intention of marrying and that she did not believe in love.

Maybe Jamie wasn't beautiful in the accepted sense of the word, but she had something more than mere beauty. Looking at her was like looking into a pool of deep, very still water; so still that you found yourself holding your breath and waiting for the faintest ripple across its smooth surface. Jamie carried with her an aura of calm and quietude, but she hadn't always been like that. Beth could remember the tomboy teenager she had been, climbing trees, running races, always covered in bruises and cuts. In those days the violet eyes had laughed, the full mouth had been mobile, her movements quicksilver.

At ten she had been desperately envious of her fourteen-year-old cousin and the closeness she shared with her stepbrother. Even though he was at university Jake had still spent a large part of his free time with his young stepsister. They had been close in a way that she as an only child had longed to imitate, but somewhere along the way something had happened to that closeness, and now...what? Now whenever she mentioned Jake in Jamie's presence, she could almost feel her cousin closing up on her, and when she mentioned Jamie to Jake his mouth would curl in that cynical way of his, his eyes as hard as chips of ice.

'Sybaritic?' Beth questioned, trying not to let Jamie see what she was thinking. 'Since when? Oh, I know you like to give that impression, Jamie, but you work hard. Too hard, Uncle Mark thinks.'

'Mark's a darling, but he's a bit old-fashioned when it comes to women. He thinks we should all be like my mother and crave only a husband, home and family.'

As she looked away from her cousin, Jamie hid her expression with long lashes that fanned her high cheekbones, giving her, although she did not know it, a look of vulnerability. Once she too had craved those things, had wanted nothing more from life than to love and be loved in return.

'Try calcium tablets.' She turned to face Beth, smiling lightly, as she firmly dismissed the past from her mind.

'Calcium tablets?' Beth looked thoroughly confused.

'For your nails,' Jamie told her, gently mockingly.

'I haven't made any plans for the weekend,' Beth told her, changing the subject. 'I thought you might fancy an early night tonight, and then tomorrow some friends of ours are coming round to dinner—I'm longing to show off my clever cousin...and Jake, of course,' Beth added absently. 'I didn't tell you, did I, that his latest girl-friend's family live only a short distance away.

'She's a nice girl—bit young for Jake, though, I would have thought. Very pretty and quite ambitious.'

Thank God she had been looking the other way, Jamie thought, as she tried to still the frantic thudding of her heart. Jake...coming here...her first impulse was to leave, immediately, but she was trapped, she knew that. If she left now Beth would guess. It was one thing for the family to know that she and Jake *disliked* each other, but...

'Jamie, are you all right? You've gone dreadfully pale.'

'Redheads are supposed to be,' Jamie told her wryly, slipping defensively behind her sophisticated mask. 'If Mark's ill, I'm surprised that Jake can spare the time to spend a weekend away.'

'Oh well, I suppose it's partly business, Amanda's father's company is merging with Brierton Plastics, apparently. That's how Jake and Amanda met. It's no secret that her parents are hoping they'll get married, but personally I think Amanda's too young—she's only nineteen, and a nice child, but somehow not what I thought Jake would choose, if you know what I mean.' She wrinkled her nose slightly and added, 'Of course, Uncle Mark would love to see him married. He and your mother complain every time I see them that you don't seem to be going to provide them with grandchildren.'

'It does seem unlikely,' Jamie agreed levelly, praying that Beth wouldn't see past her defences to what lay behind. Jake married... Pain exploded inside her, tearing her apart, making a mockery of the barriers it had taken her six years to perfect. What was the matter with her? She had known this day must come. Six years ago she had known that Jake intended to marry. He wanted a son to follow him into the business his own father had so successfully built up. Jake was both ambitious and determined. She knew that. And cruel, very, very cruel, but she was over the pain of that now. The Jake she had known and loved had never existed. That had simply been a façade which he-had hidden behind.

As she had told herself too many times over the intervening years, she told herself again that at least she had discovered the truth before it was too late, before she had been the one trapped in a marriage of ambition and greed.

She was not naïve now as she had been at eighteen, and she knew enough of the world to realise that Jake was not alone in wanting to marry for reasons advantageous to himself, but his deliberate cruelty in deceiving her into believing...

'Oh, heavens, there's the phone. Stay here and rest for a little while, I'll bring you a cup of tea.'

Alone in the guest-room Beth had given her Jamie walked over to the window and stared out across the countryside, without seeing any of its beauty. Did this girl, this Amanda, know what Jake was really like, or like her had she been deceived? That lazily mocking smile, those cool green eyes that suddenly could turn to fire, that mouth that could...

Closing her eyes to blank out her thoughts, she clung dizzily to the window ledge. Dear God, she was over this, over it. She was a different person now from the innocent trusting fool Jake had so cruelly deceived. He no longer had the power to affect her in any way at all.

So why was her heart pounding so heavily? Why was she remembering with such devastating clarity the feel of his mouth against her own?

Her only salvation when she realised the truth had been the knowledge that at least no one else knew what a fool she had been. No one else knew that they had been lovers; that Jake had whispered words of love to her and then promised to marry her, only for her to discover from his mistress that he was actually marrying her because he knew that his father was splitting his estate between the two of them; that she would have as many shares in the company as Jake himself. At first she hadn't wanted to believe Wanda's allegations, had indeed thought that the other woman was simply jealously maligning Jake; but when she had come round to his flat to tell him what had happened, the first thing she had seen as she walked in through the unlocked door had been Jake and Wanda in each other's arms.

Of course Jake had seen her, had called out to her, but she hadn't stopped, running frantically back to her car, and driving from York to Queensmeade as though the devil himself were at her heels.

Mark and her mother had been on holiday at the time—a month's holiday in Bermuda—which was why she and Jake had not said anything to anyone about their plans, wanting to save the surprise until their parents returned. She had been working on a part-time basis for a

York-based firm of interior designers, but too humiliated and hurt to face Jake she had changed her mind on reaching home, knowing that he would come after her, and instead had turned her car in the direction of the southbound motorway.

Her job didn't pay well, but she had an allowance from Mark, and enough money in her bank account to pay for a room in an inexpensive hotel for long enough for her to sort out her life.

An unaddressed letter to her employers explained to them that she wanted to work in London, and a longer, more detailed one to her parents outlined to them her plans for the future, and a third told Jake that she had made a mistake, that she wasn't ready to settle down, that she wanted her freedom and a career. She was too proud and hurt to mention Wanda.

By the time her mother and stepfather had returned from Bermuda three weeks later she had enrolled herself at classes to learn the painting techniques she now based her business on; had found herself a third-share in a flat from the notice board at the college; had had her long hair cut to shoulder length; and had totally re-vamped her wardrobe, putting away for ever the carefree coltish image of her youth, and emerging in three short weeks as the coolly sophisticated woman she was determined she was going to be.

Her parents had been a little surprised, but she had explained away the suddenness of her departure by saying that she had been torn over what to do for several months but had only finally made the decision while they were away.

They were upset at first; Mark in particular had wanted her to stay close to home. There was no need after all for her to earn her own living, and although there were many times in those early months when she would have given anything to go back, the thought of facing Jake stopped her. She had made herself a vow the evening she left his flat after discovering him with someone else that when she saw him again she would feel absolutely nothing for him—nothing at all.

The intervening six years had been busy ones. At college she had become very friendly with another student, Ralph Howard, and Ralph was now her business partner. They got on very well together, their relationship an easy undemanding one. Several of their friends thought they were or had been lovers, but that was not the case. Ralph was the brother she had never had, her relationship with him quite different from the worshipping adoration she had had for Jake.

Their hard work had paid off and now they were very successful with very busy social lives. Many of the parties they attended were business functions to which they went together. They made a striking couple, Jamie knew. Ralph was tall and blond with a year-round tan and laughing blue eyes. He looked more like a rugby player than anything else, muscular and large-boned. It always amused him to see other men treating Jamie like a fragile piece of china. At five-four with small bones and tiny narrow feet she looked far more frail than she was.

She never discouraged anyone from thinking they were lovers. It was a good way of keeping unwanted males at bay without causing offence. She knew that Ralph was curious about her sex life—or lack of it—but he respected her privacy. He knew nothing about what lay in the past. She never mentioned Jake to him, although he knew about her family background; about the marriage of her mother to her employer, then a widower with an eleven-year-old son. Beth and Richard had met Ralph. He had come to Sarah's christening with her. Jake had been godfather, but apart from one brief moment when he had held the baby and then passed her over to Jamie they had kept resolutely apart.

Her mouth curling a little, Jamie reflected that it must be rather galling to be revealed in one's true colours as Jake had been. Galling or not, it had not stopped him looking at her with cool mockery, she remembered now. Really, his arrogance was unbelievable! Had he ever thought what could have happened if she had gone to Mark and told him that his son had deliberately seduced her, deliberately allowed her to believe that he loved and wanted her, when all he wanted was her share of his father's wealth?

But she hadn't been able to do that. Both her mother and Mark adored Jake, and it would have broken Mark's heart to learn the truth. Above all else Mark was a truly honourable man, and to discover that his son was not would hurt him unbearably. So she had kept quiet, forcing herself to make for herself a new life, to give herself new motivation, to tell herself and make herself believe that what she really wanted from life was a career and success.

The late autumn dusk was fast closing to evening, reminding her how advanced the year was. The familiar pain thinking of the past always brought her was deepened by a feeling of sombre despair. It was six years ago, for God's sake, and still it was no better, all she had achieved was the ability to close herself off from the pain and pretend to the rest of the world that it simply didn't exist.

Other girls of her age endured similar traumas and recovered; went on to meet other men, make other relationships; why was it that she had never found anyone who could displace Jake from her heart?

Perhaps it was because for her the sense of betrayal had been so much greater, heightened by the fact that Jake was not only her first love and lover, but also the person closest to her in every other emotional way, so that his treachery had robbed her not only of a lover but of a brother, a friend and a secure rock to cling to all in one go.

What made it worse was the fact that she had loved him so crazily, believed in him so implicitly that she had never for one moment placed the slightest credence on Wanda's revelations. After all, she knew there had been other girls in his life before her; he was eight years older than her; he had been away at university, and above and beyond that he was a man who possessed such a powerful aura of sexual magnetism that living the life of a celibate would be practically impossible for him.

Pity the poor girl who did marry him, she thought acidly. He wouldn't remain faithful for very long, especially not to a naïve nineteen-year-old.

Although she had not seen it when they made love, looking back now she recognised that there had always been an edge of constraint in the way he touched her, a faint holding back, which she suspected now came from the fact that he had doubtless found her inexperience something of a trial. At the time she had not been aware of this, giving herself to him with a blissful joy that recognised nothing other than the unbelievable fact that he loved her. The merest touch of his fingers against her skin had been enough to set her alight with pleasure and happiness, and in her innocence she had thought it was the same for him, that the reason he had made love to her was that like her, he simply couldn't wait to consummate their love.

He had been very patient with her, very careful and gentle, but then why should he not have been, she thought bitterly now. It wouldn't have served his purpose at all for him to have frightened her away, and of course, he had always had women like Wanda to turn to for the satisfaction she didn't give him.

With a sudden shiver, she turned away from the window, achingly aware that her thoughts were careering off down a very dangerous path. She had put the past behind her, and that was where it was going to stay. Although in Jake's arms she had quivered with pleasure and ached for his touch, none of the men she had casually dated in the years that had intervened had aroused the slightest sexual interest in her. It was as though that part of her was frozen—or simply no longer existed, she thought wryly—but then what was sex after all other than simply another appetite? Did anyone waste time bemoaning the fact that they didn't long for food? Just as some people could get along with merely a couple of hours' sleep a night, while others needed eight hours, so she could live without sex. It was as simple and basic as that.

Maybe, a small inner voice criticised, but what about love? Love? Her mouth trembled and then firmed. What was love after all? That delirious, dangerous emotion Jake had aroused in her? If so she was better off without it. But she wasn't without it, she reminded herself; even the mere sound of Jake's name on someone else's lips was enough to make her muscles cramp and her pulses race. The reason she had avoided him so assiduously since she had run away was not that she loathed and hated him, but that she was terrified of betraying to his too-knowing gaze that she was still acutely vulnerable to him. Whilst he didn't know how she felt about him she felt in some indefinable way safer, although why she didn't know. After all, what difference would her feelings make to him? He had never attempted to get in touch with her, never tried to explain.

There had been a letter from him, arriving soon after he had received her note, but she had torn it up unread. Had he guessed then that she had lied when she claimed that she felt she was too young to marry and settle down? It had been little more than a sop to her pride, and she had no doubt that he had seen straight through it, but the very fact that he had made no attempt to see her or justify himself to her was surely proof of how right Wanda's allegations had been.

And now tomorrow he was coming here—with his new girlfriend. Did she have the strength to face him? Did she have any choice? If she left now Beth was bound to speculate, and she had after all nothing to fear. No one in the family knew of that brief month of ecstasy he had given her before the lies and deceit caught up with him. No, only she and Jake knew about those evenings in his flat when she had lain in his arms and felt his hands against her skin, when he had told her that he had been waiting for her to grow up, waiting for her to see him as a man and not simply as a stepbrother.

It was dark now. How long had she been standing staring into space? She glanced at her watch. Almost an hour. Beth would be wondering what on earth she was doing.

At least she had been granted a few hours to prepare herself. She looked at the case she had dropped on the bed and went over to it, unsnapping the locks. She had come straight to Bristol after nothing more than a brief stop at her London flat, giving herself time only to shower and re-pack.

In New York she had had enough free time to do some shopping. With this visit in mind she had bought a sweater for Beth and a beautifully dressed rag-doll for her goddaughter.

She unpacked automatically, her movements deft with experience. In her case was the new Calvin Klein she had bought in New York. She had packed it on impulse, a handful of dark lavender silk jersey that looked nothing on the hanger but which moulded her body and picked out the unusual colour of her eyes. It was a sophisticated dress that only just fell short of meriting the description 'sexy'. She would wear it tomorrow night, she decided grimly. Whatever her private feelings might be, she wanted Jake to be in no doubt at all that the old Jamie had gone. As she hung the dress up she thanked God for the experience that had taught her over the years exactly how to conduct a light-hearted flirtation without involving herself in anything more. If she knew her

cousin, Beth would be providing her with a dinner partner; normally she would have been cool and distant with
him, letting him know that she was not in the market for
a one-night stand or anything else, but tomorrow...

She heard her cousin's voice calling to her outside her
bedroom door, and composing her face into an expression of cool serenity she went to open it.

'Sarah's awake now,' Beth told her, holding up the
blonde-haired, blue-eyed baby for Jamie's closer inspection.

'Heavens, she's grown so much.'

After a few seconds' solemn inspection the little girl
deigned to smile.

'It's bath-time,' Beth explained, glancing ruefully at
her cousin's immaculate skirt and cashmere jumper. 'I'm
sorry to be such a poor hostess. If you want to go downstairs...'

'What I want to do,' Jamie told her firmly, 'is to help
you give my goddaughter her bath. After all,' she said
more softly, touching her fingertips to the baby's soft
skin, 'I am her godmother; which reminds me. I've
brought a small present for her from New York.'

Firmly dismissing Jake from her mind Jamie held out
her arms to take Sarah from her mother.

'Come on,' she said firmly to the little girl. 'It's time
you and I got to know one another, young lady.'

CHAPTER TWO

'JAMIE, you're an angel,' Beth said breathlessly, standing back to admire the bowl of flowers Jamie had just placed on the dining-room table.

The long velvet curtains had been closed against the dark; Jamie pursed her lips slightly as she studied her arrangement.

'With Sarah to look after I never get time for all the small details like flowers,' Beth told her wryly. 'Richard's going to get quite a shock when he finds out what we're having to eat. I'm afraid all I ever seem to manage is something simple. I really am grateful to you for everything you've done. But I feel terribly guilty. You're supposed to be here to rest.'

'I enjoyed it,' Jamie told her truthfully. 'It's been a long time since I've been let loose in a kitchen.'

'Of course, I was forgetting that your mother taught you to cook. It's no wonder you're so good.'

'Adequate but not inspired,' Jamie told her, shrugging off the compliment.

The dining-room of Beth and Richard's new house was a pleasant size but the previous owners had been less than adventurous in their choice of decor. The walls and ceiling were painted cream, taking no advantage of the lovely high ceiling and the attractive cornice.

'This room's dreadfully dull,' Beth commented critically, wrinkling her nose. 'The whole house needs redecorating, but I just don't know where to start.'

'We'll sit down tomorrow and talk about it together,' Jamie promised.

'There's Richard,' Beth exclaimed as they heard the front door open and shut.

'I'd better go upstairs and get ready,' Jamie told her, giving her cousin's husband a warm smile as he came into the room. Rather like a cuddly round teddy bear to look at, she liked Richard, who she knew was a shrewd businessman who adored his wife and little girl.

Leaving them alone together she hurried upstairs. In an hour and a half Jake would be here. Already her heart was pounding unevenly. Her fingers shook as she opened her bedroom door. She wasn't going to let seeing him affect her. She was going to be cool and indifferent to him. She had to be.

'Wow, what a stunning dress!' Beth's eyes opened wide as she studied her cousin's appearance, enviously admiring the way the silk jersey clung to Jamie's supple body. 'How on earth do you manage to stay so slim?' she complained ruefully. 'I'm at least half a stone overweight.'

'If you are that's how I like you,' Richard told his wife, coming into the kitchen behind Jamie, and going over to give Beth a quick kiss.

'Mmm, something smells good.'

'Well, you can thank Jamie. She's taken charge of tonight's meal,' Beth told him.

Jamie knew there would be eight of them altogether: Jake and his girlfriend, the local doctor and his wife, and her brother, who was apparently staying with them following a road accident, Jamie herself and Beth and Richard.

Beth had been only vaguely informative on the subject of Ian Parsons, explaining that he was a geologist who worked abroad, who had been involved in a road accident which had killed his wife.

'Ian was very badly injured, but he's on his feet again now. The accident happened over eighteen months ago, and he's been staying with Sue and Chris ever since. He's rather quiet and withdrawn,' she warned Jamie. 'Sue says he blames himself for his wife's death. They were on the verge of splitting up when it happened, and he thinks if they hadn't been arguing, his wife would never have crashed the car.'

Jamie was in the kitchen checking on the seafood crêpes she had prepared for their first course when she heard the doorbell ring.

The kitchen door was open and she heard Beth opening the door, the tiny hairs on the back of her neck prickling atavistically as she recognised the deep male drawl that answered her cousin's warm greeting. Jake had arrived!

She was glad that being in the kitchen meant that she didn't need to go out and greet them. But then wasn't that why she had offered to make the meal? She might be able to deceive others, but she couldn't deceive herself.

'Something smells good,' she heard Jake say, unconsciously repeating Richard's comment. She had forgotten that velvet, teasing quality his voice could take on. Her body was a mass of pain and she had an intense desire to open the back door and run.

Almost as though Beth had sensed it, the kitchen door was pushed open and her muscles tensed, knowing she had only seconds to prepare her defences.

All four of them walked into the room. She had her back to them as she pretended all her concentration was on what she was cooking, but in reality all she was aware of was Jake. She could almost smell the faint scent of his body, she thought feverishly, knowing by some sixth sense that he was the one standing closest to her. She *had* to turn round and face him.

'Jake.' Her smile was the perfect social widening of lips that signified politeness rather than pleasure. 'I thought I recognised your voice.'

She didn't hold her hand out to him, but gripped the spoon she was using.

He was like a force field, she thought achingly as she willed herself to meet the cool cynicism of his eyes; drawing all the energy and resistance out of her. The last time she had seen him had been at Sarah's christening, but then she made only a lightning appearance, leaving before the party afterwards with the excuse that she was due to fly to the States. Then she had had weeks to prepare herself, weeks to teach her senses to register his presence and then ignore it.

All at once she felt terribly hot and shaky. The green eyes narrowed, his glance moving slowly and thoughtfully over the silky fabric that clung to her breasts and hips.

'Doesn't Jamie look lovely?'

Even Beth seemed to be affected by the tension invading the kitchen, her voice high and slightly breathless.

Without taking his eyes off her Jake said coolly, 'She's too thin.'

He was talking about her as though she were completely incapable of emotions and feelings, and it hurt so badly she felt as though she were being ripped apart.

She mustn't let him get to her like this. Jake had always enjoyed dominating and dictating to her, she knew that, and he would enjoy doing it again, simply for the pleasure of humiliating her. She couldn't let it happen. She took a deep breath, reminding herself wryly that she was now a sophisticated businesswoman, not a mutely adoring child, and putting down the spoon she turned towards the pretty blonde girl hovering uncertainly between Jake and Beth.

'No one seems to be going to introduce us,' she said with a smile. 'I'm Jamie, and I know you must be Amanda.'

The girl, and that was exactly what she was, Jamie thought noting the clear skin and childishly rounded face, smiled back guilelessly.

'It's lovely to meet you, I've heard such a lot about you from your mother and Jake's father.'

Pain, unexpected and devastating, gripped Jamie. When Beth had talked about Jake settling down she had not really believed her, but it was obvious that Jake must have taken Amanda with him to Queensmeade.

'They're both so proud of you,' the slightly breathless voice continued, strengthening a little as she added, 'I envy you. I'd love to do something as exciting as you do.' She made a small moue. 'My father wouldn't even let me go to university. He said it was taking a place from someone else, and that I would never need to work.'

Amanda sighed, her blue eyes faintly shadowed, and against her will Jamie felt drawn to her.

The doorbell rang again, and Jamie turned back to the cooker, as Beth shepherded everyone back into the hall.

It was over and she had survived, but she couldn't relax. Her nerves were coiled into tight knots of pain.

She heard the kitchen door open again and said shakily, 'Beth, I'm afraid I have the most awful headache, would you watch the veg for me, while I run upstairs for a codeine?'

'Beth's busily organising everyone with drinks.' The laconic careless words weren't important. What was, was that Jake was here in the kitchen with her. For a moment she stood like a petrified creature, knowing that danger lurked, but too wrought up to know in what direction it might come.

'She sent me in to ask what you wanted.'

A faint grimness underlined the words.

Oh Beth, Jamie thought unhappily. You're meddling in something you don't understand.

'I think she feels that since we're both Sarah's godparents, we ought to be able to get on better together.'

Thank God she had the excuse of watching the dinner to prevent her from turning round to look at him.

He ignored her comment and said flatly instead, 'Mark's worried about you. You know he's not well?'

'Yes.' Thank goodness she had the excuse of her worry for her stepfather to excuse the tremor in her voice. 'Beth told me last night. How serious is it, Jake?'

She had to turn round to face him now, but almost flinched back as she saw the anger and contempt icing his eyes.

'Much you care,' he told her cuttingly. 'How long is it since you've been to see them, Jamie? A year, eighteen months?'

'I've been busy, I . . .'

'Rubbish!' His fingers bit into her arms as he grabbed hold of her, catching her off guard. 'You haven't come home because you can't bear to see me, isn't that closer to the truth?'

She felt she was going to choke on the pain, at the humiliation of his knowing how she felt about him, but as she looked into his eyes, it was anger she saw there and not mocking contempt.

She took a deep breath, trying to steady her nerves.

'You're being ridiculous, Jake,' she told him evenly.

'Am I? Prove it,' he challenged harshly. 'Come home for Christmas.'

The refusal rose to her lips but could not be uttered. It was six years since she had spent a Christmas at home. Six years. How she had loved their family Christmases.

'For once in your life stop being so damned selfish and put someone else first,' Jake demanded harshly. 'My father's a sick man, Jamie, he misses you.'

Blankly she looked into his face. His mouth was hard and compressed, his eyes shadowed. His hair, thick and densely black, looked as though it needed cutting. He looked tired, she recognised, momentarily stepping outside the magnetism that always held her so much in thrall and seeing him simply as another vulnerable human being. He had released her now and impulsively she wanted to reach out and touch him, to smooth away the frown creasing his forehead, and then bitterness overtook compassion. It was easy for him to condemn and criticise her. He would not have to endure the torture that would be hers if she went home, if she spent Christmas in the same house with him.

'I . . .'

'If it's me you're worried about,' he told her with cold scorn, 'then you needn't be. Mandy will be there, so you needn't worry that you might have to spend any time with me.'

'I . . .'

'Be there, Jamie,' he warned her. 'It isn't me you're punishing by staying away, you know.' His eyes darkened with anger and contempt. 'You might look the part of the sophisticated businesswoman,' he told her curtly, 'but inside you're still a spoiled petulant child.'

She watched as he left the kitchen, her throat raw with suppressed tears. How dare he speak to her like that, accuse her? Dismiss the sheer cruelty of what he had done to her as though it were nothing? He knew why she had stayed away, why she could not endure to go back to the place where she had once been so deliriously happy, but he behaved as though she were acting on nothing more than a childish whim. Punish him? Nothing she could do could do that. Did he think she didn't know it?

It was after they had finished dinner and the other guests had gone that Jake announced casually,

'By the way, has Jamie told you that she'll be coming with us to Queensmeade for Christmas this year?'

Across the space that divided them his eyes warned her against contradicting his statement. Beth was looking flushed and excited as she looked at them.

'Aunt Margaret will be so pleased. Oh, Jamie, she has missed you so much. We'll be going too, of course. You can always drive up with us if you don't fancy taking your car. I know it's two months away yet, but . . .'

'Jamie will travel with me. I have to come down to London to pick Mandy up anyway.'

In other words she wasn't going to get the opportunity to make any last-minute bid for escape, Jamie thought bitterly, avoiding looking at him.

Mandy was sitting next to her and a pleased smile curved her mouth as she listened to Jake.

'I'm so pleased you'll be coming too,' she whispered to Jamie. 'Jake can be so severe at times.' She pulled a slight face, and then coloured as she saw Jamie's surprised expression. 'My father's a very wealthy man, he doesn't consider that women can handle their financial affairs— he's old-fashioned like that. He wants me to get married and he seems to have picked on Jake as the ideal candidate. I don't suppose I should be telling you this.'

Jamie saw the slightly nervous glance she gave towards Jake who was talking to Richard.

'I like Jake, but he's very formidable, isn't he? Sometimes I feel as though he doesn't even know I'm there. And he doesn't love me.'

'Then you've nothing to worry about, have you?' Jamie said bracingly. She felt as though she had strayed into some macabre form of sick joke. Why on earth had Mandy chosen her to confide in? She looked into the younger girl's face and saw that she still looked uncertain.

'Jake wants to get married, he wants a son, a grand-child for his father, I think, and... Well, it's just that he's so very hard to argue with, isn't he?'

Oh yes, he was that all right, Jamie acknowledged to herself. Jake could be bitterly determined and stubborn when someone opposed him, and she could see how easily this young and rather diffident girl could be overwhelmed by him, especially if the marriage was something her parents approved of as well.

'I don't feel I'm mature enough to get married yet,' she confided to Jamie. 'I want to do something with my life, I don't know what yet, but I know it isn't marriage. Of course at first I was flattered when Jake showed an interest in me, but he doesn't want me really.

'I'm going to London Christmas shopping with Mummy next week. Could I come and see you? I don't have anyone I can talk to, and you are Jake's stepsister. You must know him very well.'

Well enough to know that this child wouldn't be able to withstand Jake if he turned the full force of his will and personality against her. Her common sense told her not to get involved, that it would only lead to further heartache for her. She had no wish to hear Mandy's girl-ish confidences but as she looked into the girl's agonised blue eyes she felt herself waver, and the next second she was writing down her address and telephone number, whilst at the same time wondering what on earth she was doing.

'You and Mandy seemed to be getting on very well. What do you think of her?'

Jamie hadn't needed to look over her shoulder to know that Jake was standing just behind her. That delicate personal radar that worked every time he came anywhere near her had already warned her.

She glanced across the room to where Mandy was talking to Beth before replying.

'I think she's charming,' she said shortly at last.

'The inference being far too charming for me, I take it.'

She could tell without looking at him that his mouth had twisted slightly just as she could hear the mocking amusement in his voice.

'Too charming. Too innocent, and far, far too vulnerable, Jake,' she said as coldly as she could. 'But then I'm sure you don't need me to tell you any of that. What does worry me a little is that she's also intelligent. What will you do when *she* discovers it, I wonder?'

'Bitch.' The insult was laconic, without heat or emotion. 'Still living alone, are you?'

The question was careless and uncaring, flicking her on the raw as it underlined the solitariness of her life.

'That's the way I prefer it,' she told him coldly.

'Still the ambitious career-woman. I thought it might have palled by now. Strange how I never realised all the time you were growing up that you had such a strong streak of ambition.'

'Why should you? I certainly never recognised a good many very obvious traits in you.'

He moved in front of her, frowning at the biting contempt in her voice.

'Such as?' he invited softly.

It was too much. She had already endured enough tonight, her head was pounding violently. He knew exactly what he'd done to her, so why make her say it? Did he enjoy tormenting her?

'I don't want to talk about it.' She got up too quickly, his proximity to her suddenly claustrophobic. In her panic she tried to push past him and found that his body blocked the way. Closing her eyes against the onslaught of pain in her head she swayed dangerously and put out a hand to save herself. Everything was whirling madly out of control, the only point of reality in her disordered world the sure, firm sound of Jake's voice, and she clung to it like a drowning man to a life-raft, willingly letting herself sag against his body as she felt his arms go round her and her mind abandon her completely.

Dimly she was conscious of being picked up, of being carried, of Jake's suddenly increased heartbeat. She could hear Beth asking anxious questions, and Jake's reassuringly measured reply.

'Don't worry, she always did push herself too hard. It's probably just jet-lag catching up on her. Which is her room Beth?'

And then as she closed her eyes and surrendered to the luxury of being in his arms she heard him saying, 'No, it's okay, you stay down here, I don't think she's actually fainted. More of a dizzy spell really. She'll be okay.'

They were going upstairs, Jake moving swiftly. He had carried her like this once before, the first time he had made love to her. All at once her stomach clenched on a fierce burst of pain. She didn't want to remember that time now. How thrilled and yet frightened she had been, how gentle and tender Jake's lovemaking. But it was pointless remembering it, it had all only been an illusion, something deliberately created to deceive, and neither her pride nor her self-respect had ever recovered from the fact that it had deceived, very successfully.

Indeed if it hadn't been for Wanda she would never have found out, would now have been married to Jake for five years, would probably be the mother of his children. So why didn't she feel relief instead of dull misery? Would she really have preferred not to know, to have married him anyway? Angered by her own weakness, she tried to push the memories away. They were inside her bedroom now. She opened her eyes cautiously, hurriedly closing them again as she felt the room sway. It was her own fault, she thought guiltily, she had eaten next to nothing on the flight from New York, and very little since. No wonder she had no strength, no resistance.

Past and present started to merge dizzily together, loosening her hold on reality, confusing her to the point where she wasn't sure of anything other than the fact that she was in Jake's arms. She felt him lower her on to the bed, and opened her eyes, blinking as she was caught in the cool green beam of his.

'Jake.'

Her whole body trembled with the effort of speaking his name, weak tears almost blinding her as she saw that she had been unsuccessful in banishing the hard coldness from his eyes. She was eighteen again and desperately in love. She reached out, imploring, her breath ejected from her lungs in a shocked whimper as Jake drew back, holding her away so savagely she thought he might crush her fragile bones.

'What is it you want from me, Jamie?'

His voice had an unfamiliar raggedness to it, a harsh echo of an old pain that disturbed and confused her. Her tongue touched the dry contours of her mouth, her stomach cramping in nervous protest. She felt light-headed and dizzy, unable to formulate any words that would make any sense. Somewhere at the back of her mind trembled a warning that she was doing something incredibly foolish, but she was not prepared to listen to it. All she could think of was how much she ached and yearned for this man sitting beside her, and looking at her as though for some reason he wanted to strangle her.

Confusion hazed her mind, trapping her back in the past, her eyes unknowingly eloquent and pleading as she looked at him.

'Jamie, for God's sake.' His fingers snapped back from her wrists as though her skin burned. 'What in hell's name are you playing at now?'

He was moving away from her and she didn't want him to go. Panic and pain tore at her with knife-sharp claws, a whirling black emptiness was engulfing her, through which she cried out his name in sharp anguish.

Momentarily the darkness parted and she felt the heat of Jake's body against her own, his mouth on hers, swiftly answering the plea in her voice. Mindlessly, voluptuously she gave herself up to the pleasure of touching and kissing him, her tongue feverishly tracing the well remembered shape of his lips, her heart thudding frantically against her ribs.

'Jamie?'

The sound of Beth's hesitant voice brought her abruptly awake. Confused, she glanced around, stunned to discover that it was daylight. 'How are you feeling?' Beth approached the bed anxiously. 'I wanted to call the doctor last night, but Jake said it wasn't necessary. He says you had a bout of these fainting attacks during your teens.'

'Yes, I did,' she responded almost absently, her mind struggling to assimilate the bewildering confusion of images and half-memories surging through her. Jake had carried her upstairs last night, he had been angry with her, they had argued; her face flamed hotly as she had a sudden, too-vivid memory of something else. Her mind must be playing tricks on her. She couldn't have really kissed him . . . She closed her eyes, shuddering slightly.

'Jamie.'

'I'm fine, just a little weak . . .'

'Jake said you were asleep when he left you. He told me not to disturb you last night. It's just as well he was here. I had no idea you were subject to these attacks.'

Jamie wanted to tell her that she wasn't, that her faintness had been brought on by a headache and the acute tension engendered by Jake's presence, but wisely she said nothing. Her heart was still pounding fiercely, her thoughts tormented by that hazy memory of Jake's mouth against her own as she used all the skill he had taught her to soften its hard outline. Dear God, surely she could not have done such a thing? It must surely be her imagination playing tricks on her. How on earth was she ever going to face Jake again if . . .

Other memories began to surface. Jake had tricked her into agreeing to go home at Christmas. But why? He could want her company as little as she wanted his. He had claimed that Mark and her mother missed her. Her mouth tightened. Was that why he wanted her there, or was it simply so that he could torment her further?

'What did you think of Amanda?' Beth asked eagerly, sitting down on the edge of the bed, as Jamie struggled to sit up. 'She's nice, isn't she?'

'Far too nice for Jake,' Jamie replied promptly, wishing she hadn't been so curt when she saw Beth's surprised expression. 'She was telling me last night that she isn't at all keen on the idea of getting married yet, to anyone,' she told Beth by way of explanation. 'I get the impression she's scared stiff that between them her father and Jake will force her into it.'

'Oh no, surely not? Jake would never do anything like that. Why, if he wants to get married he could find any number of women who'd jump at the chance.'

'Ex-mistresses, you mean?' Jamie said sarcastically. 'Jake's too proud for that, Beth. He'll want a wife he can mould and dominate. An innocent, untainted by any other man sexually or mentally. I'm sure in his eyes Amanda would make him an excellent wife. She's an only child and her father is a very wealthy man.'

'I know you and Jake don't get on, but surely that isn't really how you see him, is it?' Beth was plainly troubled. 'I know he can be strong-willed and arrogant, but . . .'

'No buts, Beth,' Jamie told her wearily. 'Jake's cool-headed enough to decide what he wants out of life and then to go out and get it without bothering himself over trivial little details like emotions and feelings.'

Plainly perplexed by her cousin's bitterness, Beth stood up. 'I just came to see if you were awake. I'll go and make you a cup of tea now. Are you sure you're feeling all right?'

Nodding her head, Jamie turned her face into the pillow. All right was the last thing she felt. No amount of determination had protected her from the savage reality of seeing Jake. It was the same every time and it got worse, not better. She shuddered as she tried to eject from her mind the tormentingly hazy memory of being in his arms; of wantonly pressing herself up against his body, of betraying herself to him in the most humiliating way possible. Sweat broke out on her forehead, sickness cramping through her stomach. Please God, let it not be true, let that mocking elusive memory belong to the more distant past, or better still her imagination. She could not, would not endure the torment of Jake knowing that her years of cool indifference towards him were nothing more than a brittle barrier behind which she hid her love.

CHAPTER THREE

ANOTHER day over—thank God. Sighing faintly, Jamie locked the door of the office behind her and hurried out into the cold early November darkness.

They had been busy recently, but that was not the reason for the lines of tension creasing her forehead and the overstrained look in her eyes. Even Ralph, her partner, had commented that she was not her normal cool, calm self. She had Jake to thank for that, she thought angrily, her soft mouth twisting.

Only last week she had received an ecstatic letter from her mother telling her how thrilled she and Mark were that she was going to be able to get home for Christmas—Jake had told them, apparently.

Trust him. He was tying her up in knots, making it impossible for her to find an excuse for not going home. How ill was Mark? A deeper frown touched her forehead. Whenever she asked her mother about her stepfather the replies she received were reassuring but evasive. Very mild angina was how her mother had described Mark's condition, but what if it were more than that, what if... Panic and dread clutched her heart at the thought of anything happening to her stepfather, if he was more seriously ill than she was being told and something should happen to him. She knew that she would never forgive herself if Mark died without her having seen him.

Even so the situation was an impossible one. If only Jake did not live so close to Queensmeade. Because he had taken over the running of the factory he was constantly in and out of Queensmeade discussing business with his father, and unless she knew specifically that he was going to be away she had purposely not gone home, unable to bear the thought of facing him in the place where she had once known such foolish joy.

How typical it was of Jake's arrogance that he should expect her to put the past calmly behind her and behave as though nothing had happened. If Wanda hadn't opened her eyes to the truth she would have been married to him and it would have been too late. They had planned to tell Mark and her mother how they felt about one another on their return from holiday. Jake had been talking about a Christmas wedding. How naïve she had been to think he actually loved her, and how clever he had been to keep her in the dark as to his real feelings.

What hurt her most was not that she had loved him, but that she had trusted him as well, had looked up to him and adored him all through their childhood—and been too bedazzled by the wonder of this demigod, whom she had worshipped all her life, actually loving her, to have the wit to question the reality of an experienced and very male man in his mid-twenties falling passionately in love with an inexperienced teenager he had known all his life.

But if Wanda had not told her would she have been any better off? she wondered cynically, dodging down into the underground. She enjoyed her work—when she was working—but the PR side of the business, so necessary to keep commissions rolling in, was something she preferred to leave to Ralph. Wouldn't she have been equally content to run the business as a small and probably only marginally profitable sideline, occupying most of her time as Jake's wife and the mother of his children?

She was not ambitious and never had been, which did not mean that she thought of herself as in any way inferior or subservient to any man. Her mother had shown her that it was possible for a woman to be all those things that were 'feminine' and yet to retain her independence and self-worth at the same time. She had seen for herself that for all his wealth and power Mark was as dependent on her mother as she was on him, perhaps more so. Any emotions one felt for another human being to some extent made one vulnerable, dependent. Some of her female acquaintances would have a field-day if they could read her mind, she thought wryly, as she stepped off the train and joined the surge of fellow commuters pressing up the escalators.

The wind had picked up since she had left the office and it whipped icily at her exposed ankles as she hurried towards her small Victorian house. She had bought it with the small amount of money her father had left her, when it had been in a dilapidated and very run-down state. Now five years later it was an undeniable advertisement for the company's work.

She let herself into the small hall and snapped on the lights. The plain French-blue carpet soothed her eyes, the soft butter-yellow dragged walls banishing the cold dampness of the November night.

Because the house was small she had opted for the same colour-scheme throughout, taking advantage of her knowledge of all the different paint finishes to achieve contrasting effects in each room.

As always, the first thing she did when she got home was to go upstairs to her bedroom, to shed the formality of her coolly efficient business suit.

Like the rest of the house the room was decorated in yellows and French-blues, but in this room the yellow was toned down to buttermilk, the creamy glazed cotton fabric that covered the bed and windows sprigged with small flowers. Draped curtains hung from a circlet in the ceiling to frame the bedhead, both curtains and bedspread edged in a plain blue fabric that matched the carpet exactly. Jamie had spent weeks hunting for that particular shade of blue, and she was very pleased with the effect, although she knew her bedroom hinted at a more frivolous and feminine personality than most people thought she had.

On one wall, fitted wardrobes were cleverly concealed by panels covered in the floral fabric, the wall-lights casting a warm golden glow on the room.

The house only had two bedrooms but each had its own bathroom. Jamie had opted for plain golds and yellows in hers to tone in with her bedroom, while the guest-room had a rather more ambitious traditional Victorian brass and mahogany decor that suited the high-ceilinged room.

Her evening ritual was always the same, and it struck her as she took off her clothes and quickly showered that she was becoming set in her ways, old-maidish almost. Shrugging the thought aside—she had no desire to marry—she dried herself and dressed again in a bright green tracksuit.

Downstairs in the kitchen she prepared herself a snack of scrambled eggs and a mug of coffee, taking it on a tray into the small study-cum-sitting-room at the back of the house.

Curling up into a comfortable easy chair, she ate her supper, absently watching television.

It was only here in her own domain that she was able to relax, but even here she didn't feel as safe as she once had. Safe? The thought made her frown. What on earth was she frightened of? Jake? There was no need, surely. All right, so he was forcing her to go home for Christmas, but not for his benefit. Jake had no desire for her company. She had nothing to fear from him in either the emotional or the sexual sense because she already knew he didn't want her.

No, what she had to fear was herself, she acknowledged wryly. That and her dread that she would not be able to keep her feelings for him to herself if she was forced into his company too often. That was the real reason she could not go home, it had nothing to do with resentment or dislike, and everything to do with the fact that no matter how much she tried, she simply could not dislodge him from her heart.

She was just on the point of deciding she would have an early night when the front doorbell rang.

Since she was not expecting anyone she frowned, a mental image of Jake flashing through her brain, as though somehow by thinking about him she had conjured him up outside her door.

Only it wasn't Jake who faced her when she opened the door. It was Amanda, and she barely had time to recognise her sharp disappointment before the younger girl erupted into a frantic plea to be allowed to come in.

As she automatically stepped back, Jamie's eyes widened as she took in the girl's soaking jeans and jacket. Her blonde hair was plastered to her skull. Remembering her suggestion that she come and visit her while she and her mother were shopping, for a moment Jamie was nonplussed by the younger girl's appearance. From what she had learned of Amanda's parents, she didn't think her mother was the sort of woman who would take her daughter out shopping dressed in faded jeans and an old anorak.

'I had to come. There wasn't anywhere else.' A shiver interrupted the frantic high-pitched words, and Jamie felt her initial astonishment harden into sharp unease. Now that she looked more closely she saw that Amanda was close to hysteria, alternately shivering and crying.

Gently she led her into the study, sitting her down by the fire while she went upstairs to get clean warm towels.

'Dry your hair and get out of those wet things,' she instructed calmly, handing her a towelling robe and the towels. 'I'll go and make us both a cup of coffee.'

By the time she came back with the two mugs, Amanda was huddled in front of the fire in the robe. As she handed her her coffee Jamie saw how her fingers trembled. She had lost weight too, she thought, studying her, and there was a tension in her blue eyes that hadn't been there before.

'I take it that you aren't in London shopping with your mother,' she said wryly, sitting down opposite her.

Amanda shot her a look of guilty despair before shaking her head. 'No. I've . . . I've left home.'

Left home! Why on earth should she be so surprised? Jamie wondered ironically. She ought to have guessed the moment she opened the door to her.

'I see.' She was thinking quickly. 'Do your parents know where you are?'

Again Amanda shook her head. 'No. And I don't want them to know, otherwise they'll come for me and my father will make me marry Jake.'

More tears fell, while Jamie tried to assimilate this last bombshell.

'Make you . . .'

'Yes. We had the most terrible argument about it last week. I like Jake, Jamie, but I don't want to marry him. I don't want to marry anyone yet, I want to be free, to travel, to make something of myself. My father just can't see that I don't want to be a pampered, cushioned doll like my mother. I'm not that sort, I want to be independent.'

'Well, I can understand that,' Jamie soothed, privately wondering how on earth Amanda's father had managed to be so stupid as to panic his daughter into flight.

'I know you've told me why your father is so keen for you to marry Jake,' she said quietly, 'but Amanda, it isn't up to him, you know. Jake does have some say in this, and I can't honestly see him forcing you into a marriage you don't want.'

'That's what I thought,' Amanda agreed miserably, 'but last night when I tried to tell him how I felt all he kept talking about was how much he needed a wife, how much he wanted to provide his father with a grandson.' She shuddered. 'It was awful, Jamie. I'd always liked him before, even quite...' She blushed a little. 'Well, been quite attracted to him—he's so different from the other boys I've been out with. For one thing he can stand up to my father, but when he started talking about the sort of wife he wanted, the kind of life she would lead...' She shuddered again. 'It was positively Victorian!'

'Did you tell him about the pressure your father's putting on you?'

'I was going to, but then I couldn't. I can't marry him, Jamie. I don't want to. There was no one else I could go to. I had to come to you.' Fresh tears spurted. Jamie looked at her down-bent head, her heart filled with bitterness. How could Jake contemplate marriage with this child? And a child was exactly what Amanda was.

'Please, let me stay here!'

'I don't see that I've any choice,' Jamie told her drily. 'I can hardly turn you out into the night, can I?'

She was rewarded with an impulsive hug. 'I knew you'd understand.' Jamie permitted herself a wintry smile.

'You can stay tonight, Amanda, but tomorrow we'll have to let your parents know where you are. They'll be worried about you,' she told her. Privately she felt that if Amanda's parents couldn't see before how immature and unready for marriage their daughter was, her running away must surely tell them.

'They'll make me go back and marry Jake.'

'Not necessarily,' Jamie told her, reminding her calmly, 'you *are* over eighteen, after all.'

'Will you talk to them, Jamie?' Amanda pleaded. 'You could make them understand. They'd listen to you.'

Would they? Jamie doubted it, but seeing that her un-expected guest was close to hysteria again, she said soothingly, 'When we let them know where you are to-morrow, I'll suggest that they come here, and...'

'And then you'll tell them that I don't want to marry Jake?'

'No. *You'll* tell them that, Amanda,' she said firmly, and then taking a deep breath added recklessly, 'but don't forget you are over eighteen and if you feel that they'll persist in trying to coerce you into marriage with him— well, I have a spare bedroom here and...'

'You mean I can come and live with you here, in Lon-don?'

Wondering what on earth she had let herself in for, Jamie reiterated firmly, 'We'll talk about it all tomor-row.'

By the time she had washed the coffee-mugs it was eleven o'clock and despite her denials it was obvious that Amanda was tired. It wouldn't do her parents any harm to worry about her for one night, Jamie decided hard-heartedly, and besides, she didn't really think she could face an irate parent at this time of night.

As she rummaged through her wardrobe to find nightclothes and a clean pair of jeans for the morning, she asked thoughtfully, 'How did you get to London, Amanda?'

There was a brief pause which caused her to look searchingly at her young guest. Amanda looked both guilty and defiant. 'I hitched a lift,' she said at last.

Jamie went cold inside. She was even more of a rebel-lious child than she had thought. How could Jake even contemplate marrying her? She would never make the sort of conventional, docile child-bride he had looked for in her; never.

'You needn't look at me like that,' Amanda cried defensively. 'He was a perfectly nice man. I could tell.'

'Could you?' The intensity of her own anger startled Jamie. 'And if he hadn't been, Amanda? Or would that simply have been another way of punishing your parents?'

She had the grace to blush, her expression faintly sulky, as she plucked nervously at the belt of her robe.

'Well, it's not up to me to lecture you,' Jamie admitted drily. 'At least you're here and safe. Try and get some sleep, and then tomorrow morning I'll speak to your parents.'

What on earth was she letting herself in for? Jamie wondered as she slid into her own bed. She felt immeasurably older than Amanda, and it wasn't simply overwhelming, intense jealousy that made her feel that she wasn't the right wife for Jake. Jake... He wouldn't thank her for interfering in his affairs, she recognised on a sudden shiver of alarm, but what alternative did she have? She could hardly turn Amanda out, nor would her own conscience allow her simply to pack her off back to her parents, without making some attempt to help her.

'Hi, I've brought you some coffee.'

The sight of Amanda sitting on the side of her bed, her blonde hair caught up in bunches, her expression happy and relaxed, made Jamie lean up on one elbow as the events of the previous evening filtered back. Oh, for the recuperative powers of the very young, she thought wryly as she surveyed her visitor.

'What time is it?' She grimaced as she saw her watch. 'I'll have to ring my office and tell them that I won't be in today, and then,' she fixed Amanda with a firm look, 'we're going to ring your parents.'

The distraught sob of relief with which Caroline Farmer greeted the news that her daughter was safe and well fanned Jamie's guilt for keeping the information from her overnight. Across the room from her Amanda sat watching her, her eyes shadowed and wary, and when Jamie asked if she might speak to Amanda's father, real apprehension shadowed their blue depths.

Over the years Jamie had grown used to dealing with angry, intimidating men, and her cool, crisp voice soon cut through Gerald Farmer's tirade of fury.

Coolly she explained to him exactly why his daughter had sought refuge with her, adding that she felt it would benefit them all if he and Amanda's mother could make the trip to London so that the whole subject could be discussed.

There was a good deal more furious bombardment from the man on the other end of the line, as he demanded to know what business it was of Jamie's.

'None at all,' she told him icily. 'But I could remind you that Amanda is an adult, and that I have offered her a home with me should she feel unable to return to you.'

'She hasn't a penny of her own, and she'll get nothing from me!'

'That's all right,' Jamie told him, cutting through his bluster. 'I'm both able and willing to support her financially while she trains for a job.'

The conversation was concluded with his grudging agreement to come to the house later in the morning.

'You were fantastic,' Amanda applauded. 'So cool and calm. I wish I could be like you. Will you really let me stay here?'

Privately Jamie hoped it wouldn't come to that. Beneath Gerald Farmer's furious bluster she had sensed a very real love for his daughter, and if he could be brought to see that a daughter could make as able a business lieutenant as a son, Jamie suspected that the whole problem could be resolved to everyone's satisfaction. Excepting Jake, of course. Jake would not be at all pleased at having his prospective bride snatched away from him.

'Your parents will be here within a couple of hours,' she told Amanda, 'and I suggest you spend that time drawing up some concrete plans to put in front of your father. You say you want to be independent and have your own career, Amanda. Prove it to him. Write down what your ambitions are and how you hope to fulfil them. Show him that you are capable of managing your own life.'

Four hours later, mentally exhausted but considerably relieved, Jamie stood by her sitting-room window and watched as Amanda and her parents drove away.

The meeting between parents and daughter had gone much as she had anticipated, but Amanda's calmly determined manner had eventually cut through her father's paternal anger, and he had grudgingly agreed to sit down and listen to what she had to say.

Jamie had simply sat in on the discussion in silence, ready to intervene if Amanda asked for help, but otherwise merely an observer. As she had pointed out to Amanda before her parents' arrival, her father would be much more convinced of her maturity if she put her own points and arguments across rather than relying on Jamie to do it for her.

As Jamie had suspected, like many successful and dominant people Amanda's father responded best to those who stood up to him, and she could see that although he tried hard to conceal it, he was secretly proud and impressed by his daughter's calm determination.

It was only after they had driven away that Jamie's thoughts turned to Jake's part in the proceedings. Without Amanda's father's backing he would find it impossible to force Amanda into marriage, and he would be very angry when he discovered the part she had played in the proceedings.

That tingle of sensation that ran down her spine could surely not be fear? Unlike Amanda's father Jake rarely raised his voice; he never needed to, she reflected nervously, a simple look from those icy eyes could be so devastatingly blighting that it wasn't necessary. Her chin lifted a little. The days were gone when she had been accountable to Jake, but as she turned away from the window, she couldn't help remembering how she had felt when Amanda told her that Jake wanted to marry her.

It was stupid to feel jealous. After all, *she* could have been his wife had she wanted to be; and Amanda's role in his life would have been exactly the same as hers. He hadn't professed to love the younger girl. But he *had* claimed to love *her*.

Compressing her lips firmly, Jamie walked into her kitchen and started washing the coffee-cups. Her intelligence told her that she had done the right thing in walking out on Jake all those years ago, in refusing to see him or answer his letter when he had found out where she was—in refusing to accept a marriage made for cynical and worldly reasons alone, but emotionally...ah, that was a different story. Emotionally she was still as vulnerable to him as she had always been, which was why she always fought so hard against seeing him, which was why she was dreading this Christmas visit home so much.

Had she helped Amanda for purely altruistic reasons, or had she been, partially at least, motivated by jealousy?

What did it matter? Amanda had decided against marrying Jake before she had come to her for help. But would Jake see it that way? she wondered uneasily. Amanda's father had promised to see Jake and make it plain to him that he was not going to coerce his daughter into a marriage she did not want, and Jamie suspected it was too much to hope that the Farmers would refrain from mentioning her own part in the proceedings, which meant that sooner or later Jake was going to try to exact retribution for what he would undoubtedly see as her interference in his life.

Come on, what's the matter with you? she demanded of herself. You're not afraid of him. What can he do? He's only a man.

Only a man...her own words seemed to mock her, for the lies she knew they were. Only a man perhaps, but where she was concerned Jake was The Man, the one and only, and if she hadn't realised it before, that last weekend at Beth's had proved it to her.

She only had to see him for her self-control to shatter and her senses to respond outrageously to his presence. The physical desire he had aroused in her at eighteen seemed to have grown over the years rather than diminished.

Celibacy was not a good thing, she decided wryly; it tended to concentrate the mind too much. She might have done better to take a string of lovers, but she had always been too fastidious for that, ridiculously so when she remembered the intense physical passion Jake had been able to arouse in her. Funny that she could be so passionate with one man and yet so cold with all the others. It was a quirk in her nature that irritated her, and one she was normally able to keep carefully concealed from herself—that was until she actually had to face Jake in the flesh. Then it had all been there: the heavy heartbeat; the inner tension; the too-sensitive skin that ached for his touch.

Work, she told herself firmly as she finished drying the cups. Work was the panacea, the pain-blocker. Work, work and more work.

CHAPTER FOUR

'WHAT on earth's got into you this last week?' Ralph complained mock-seriously. 'You're working like there's no tomorrow.'

'A sudden energy drive,' Jamie told him, bending her head over the work schedules spread out on her desk. 'You know how it is, people want work completed before Christmas.'

'I know how it is,' Ralph agreed, 'but I've never seen you like this before. You're all hyped up, so much so that you're beginning to worry me. You need to relax, Jamie. If you don't...' He shook his head, and looked at her shrewdly. 'My guess is that it's some sort of man trouble.'

'Mind your own business.'

He accepted her rebuff with a faint grin. 'Aha, so I'm right! Welcome to the human race, my love. I was beginning to think you were a-human. Who is he? Do I know him?'

'If we juggle these two contracts around, we should be able to fit the Bensons in the week after next, they...'

'Aha, I see, so I'm not going to be told, is that it? Mmmm, must be serious, then.' He glanced at his watch. 'Hope you've remembered it's the Johnsons' cocktail party tonight. We promised to put in an appearance.'

Jamie frowned slightly. She had forgotten, although Ralph was quite right. They had promised to attend the house-warming party being thrown by the young couple who had commissioned them to decorate their Chelsea house. Howard Johnson worked for one of the independent TV companies and his wife Elena was in advertising. They had both been thrilled by the work she and Ralph had done for them, and Jamie knew that the evening could well lead to new business. Even so, she was conscious of a desire to suggest that Ralph went alone.

'Oh no, you don't,' he cautioned her, accurately reading her thoughts. 'This is business, my love, and business comes first, remember? You were the one who said so. Look,' he said in a more serious voice, 'we both ought to go, the Johnsons will be offended if we don't.'

'Umm, they want to show us off as a new discovery.'

Shrugging lightly at her caustic tone, Ralph eyed her thoughtfully. 'Well, that's the way the business is, love, you know that. And you've never minded before.'

'I know. I'm sorry if I'm griping, it's just that I feel rather tired.'

'Burning the candle at both ends?' he suggested drily, but although he had accused her of having a man in her life he could see no signs of the physical satisfaction he would have expected in her face. On the contrary, she looked strained and exhausted; she had lost weight, he noted absently, her whole body radiating a stressed tension that reminded him of a bow too tightly drawn. Something was wrong, but he knew Jamie well enough to know that she would not confide in him. That was not her way.

If she had fallen in love with someone, it wasn't bringing her any pleasure. A married man perhaps? But no, that wasn't her style. It struck him then how little he knew about her private life, despite the years they had worked together.

'Want me to call for you tonight?' he suggested. 'Save you driving?'

'Thanks, I must admit I don't feel up to coping with London traffic at the moment.'

'That's what partners are for,' he told her with a smile, brushing aside her thanks. 'Pick you up at seven-thirty?' He glanced at his watch again. 'Look, it's half four now. Why don't you call it a day, and go home and rest for a while. There's nothing more you can do here now. The schedules are all up to date, and...'

'I was going to write to the Spencers and the Fortunes, confirming the dates for starting work with them.'

'*I'll* do it,' Ralph told her firmly. 'You get yourself home. It won't do the business any good if you turn up at the Johnsons' tonight looking the way you do right now.'

She knew that he was right. The media-set amongst which the Johnsons moved were very image-conscious, and although the company was doing well, they could not afford to lose possible business.

Instead of going straight back to her flat, on a sudden impulse she called in instead at the Mayfair hairdressers, where she went for her regular six-weekly trim.

She was in luck and her stylist had a free appointment. When Jamie told him she wanted a change he pursed his lips slightly and studied her for a moment.

'Not short,' he said firmly, 'but something younger, freer.'

An hour later when Jamie emerged from the salon, she wasn't sure whether she had done the right thing or not.

Her hair had been cut to shoulder length in a smooth elegant bob, but the hair on top of her head had been cut short and gelled to give an informal, very casual and breezy youthfulness to the hairstyle. When she had queried doubtfully whether the style wasn't a bit young for her, the stylist had laughed at her, commenting that her previous style had been too old.

In her determination to carve an independent career for herself and free herself from the humiliation of accepting marriage to Jake simply because there was nothing else she could do, she had been forced to grow up quickly. In those early years of forming the business there had been no time for play. She was after all still only twenty-four, she reminded herself as she headed for her flat. So why was it that she felt so much older? She was successful and independent with the whole of her life ahead of her, so why did she feel so empty and drained? Why couldn't she fight free of this terrible longing for Jake? She didn't regret her decision not to marry him, but a tiny part of her couldn't help thinking how different her life might have been had she never discovered the truth about why he was marrying her. But she had discovered it, she told herself firmly as she let herself into her flat. She had discovered it and had made the only decision possible in the circumstances. In doing so she had saved her self-respect and broken her heart.

Ralph arrived to pick her up dead on seven-thirty, his eyes widening appreciatively as he took in her new hairstyle and the highly fashionable outfit she was wearing. The thin supple jersey clung provocatively to her body, the subtle pinky-gold colour magically underlining the richness of her hair.

'Wow, what happened to the tired lady who left the office this afternoon?'

'Like it, then?' She touched her hair slightly self-consciously.

'I'd show you how much, but it would make us late for the party,' he told her with a grin.

They had always been good friends without anything sexual between them, and when Jamie flashed him a warning look, he held up his hands and said, 'Okay, okay, I know I'm the brother you never had, but tonight you look one hell of a sexy lady, Jamie, and I'm not going to be the only man to think so.'

'A new hairstyle and outfit suddenly turns me into a sex-bomb, is that what you're trying to tell me?' she scoffed.

Ralph shook his head. 'Not exactly, let's just say the potential's always been there, but this is the first time I've seen you underline it. Something's happened to you recently, Jamie. I'm not sure what or who it is, but I'll tell you one thing. Tonight when men ask for your telephone number, it won't just be because they want you to paint their walls.'

'I'm twenty-four, not sixteen, Ralph,' she told him coolly, 'and perfectly capable of sorting out the sheep from the wolves.'

'You reckon.' His glance was wry. The warning look she gave him stopped him from going any further.

As he opened the door of his car for her, he sighed faintly. Jamie meant a lot to him. There had been a time when they first met when he had hoped for more from their relationship, but over the years he had come to look on her as more of a friend and business partner than a woman. Tonight, totally unexpectedly, his old desire for her had suddenly surfaced and he felt an angry spiral of resentment flare inside him at her obvious indifference. Quenching it, he got into the car and started the engine. Jamie was out of bounds to him, she always had been and she always would be, but it was obvious to him that there was someone who managed to get through to her. Who was he?

The party was in full swing when they arrived, and the moment she saw the elegance of the other female guests, Jamie realised that her hair stylist had been right. Women a lot older than her sported a wide variety of youthfully modern hairstyles.

Howard Johnson had opened the door to them and now he was shuffling through the crowd in the direction of the bar.

'Let me get you both a drink and then I'll introduce you around. Almost everyone else here knows one another. Elena,' he called across to his wife, who was chatting animatedly in the centre of one group, 'Jamie and Ralph are here.'

Elena Johnson broke off her conversation to come over to them. She kissed Jamie slightly theatrically on one cheek, her kiss for Ralph noticeably warmer than mere convention demanded.

Watching Ralph respond enthusiastically to her encouragement, Jamie wondered a little bitterly if all men were the same: opportunists, selfishly egotistical.

A glass of champagne was thrust into her hand as Howard propelled her away from Ralph and into the group of people he had just left.

Introductions were made, so quickly that she could catch no more than one or two names; the doorbell rang and Howard left her. The conversation around her was almost exclusively media-orientated, the pace slightly frenetic. Sipping her champagne, Jamie was content simply to stand on the sidelines and absorb everything that was going on around her.

'Ready to make tracks?' Ralph's voice at her shoulder proved a welcome interruption to the monologue she had been enduring. Breaking into her companion's petulant criticism of the interior designer she had hired to do her bedroom, Jamie excused herself.

'Thanks for rescuing me,' she murmured to Ralph as they went to look for their hosts.

'Umm, I thought I saw a rather glazed look in your eyes.' His arm protected her from another guest pushing past, its bulk solid and warm against her. His automatic reaction was the natural male one, the touch of his fingers against her skin affecting her not at all, but if Jake had touched her like that... Why on earth was she destroying herself like this, constantly thinking about him, tormenting herself? She had made her decision six years ago, and she ought to be over him by now.

In fact she thought she was until she had seen him at the christening and then again the other weekend.

'Where do you go when you get that look in your eyes?' Ralph quizzed her as they went outside.

When she shook her head, he shrugged his shoulders slightly. 'Okay, keep it to yourself if you want to, but you can't fool me, Jamie. Something or someone's bothering you.'

While he drove her home he chatted about the evening and the people they had met, apparently not put off by her monosyllabic responses. As he stopped his car outside her flat Jamie noticed another one parked several yards away.

'Mmm, nice,' commented Ralph, glancing at it, 'one of the new BMWs. You've got some wealthy neighbours.'

Instead of getting out of the car he turned slightly towards her, catching her off guard as he drew her into his arms, feathering her mouth with his own before she could protest.

Ralph was an attractive man, and Jamie had noticed more than one woman eyeing him thoughtfully during the course of the evening, but in his arms she felt nothing at all, no excitement, no desire, nothing.

As his body registered her lack of desire he released her unhurriedly, frowning slightly as they looked at one another.

'Not a good idea,' he commented ruefully, pushing his fingers through his hair, in an oddly boyish gesture. 'I suppose I ought to have known better.'

'Much better,' Jamie confirmed drily, wondering as she did so why on earth she couldn't feel equally indifferent to Jake. Ralph was an experienced and attractive man, a man any woman could enjoy as a lover, but he simply aroused nothing within her at all. It was as though once she had been touched by Jake he had put some spell on her which made it impossible for her to respond to any other man, and hard as she had tried in the past to break free of that unwanted enchantment, it was impossible.

'I'll go in.' She made to get out of the car, letting Ralph take her arm as he escorted her to the door of her flat.

'Still friends?' he asked whimsically.

'Friends,' Jamie agreed, leaning forward to give him a quick kiss on the cheek before unlocking her door.

As she went inside and switched on the light, the mirror in the small hallway threw back her reflection, its unfamiliarity momentarily shocking her. She touched her hair, frowning slightly, her own image in the mirror fading to be replaced by the shockingly gut-wrenching memory of Jake winding her hair round his fingers and then watching it spill through his hands as they made love. The shock of the too-intrusive memory was sickening, her whole body shivering as it reacted with feverish eagerness to the memory of how she had felt when he touched her.

As always when she thought about those weeks when they had been lovers she was shamed by her own inability to remain unaffected by her memories. She was a fool. She should have found another lover to take Jake's place straight away and then she wouldn't suffer like this. The trouble was that she had no one to compare with him, no yardstick against which to measure the pleasure he had given her. And now it seemed it was too late. She had thought herself beyond the need for sex, free of the fierce burn of intense desire, but the truth had been brought home to her the day of the christening, when just to see him had been to unleash a fierce agony of need.

The doorbell rang, and she swung round, automatically opening the door.

'Ralph, what . . .' The words died, her mouth opening in shock as she stared at the man framed in the doorway. 'Jake!'

'So, you *do* remember my name?' His mouth twisted mockingly as he walked into her house. 'Seems so long since I've heard you say it I had begun to wonder.'

'What . . . what are you doing here?'

She saw his eyebrows lift and the heat that seared her stomach when she first saw him turned to ice. She had been so caught up in the past that she had almost forgotten the present.

'Amanda,' she said flatly, answering her own question.

'Exactly.' The door swung closed behind him, and she moved automatically into the sitting-room, knowing he was right behind her.

'You're lucky to find me in,' she told him caustically, fighting to recover from the shock of seeing him. 'I've been out all evening.'

'I know.' His voice was dry, but tinged with something else. What? Anger, most likely, Jake would not like having to hang about, he never had.

'I saw you arrive back. Not exactly passionate, is he?'

She swung round, her eyes widening at the implication in his voice, and then she lowered her head, concealing her thoughts from him. So he thought she and Ralph were lovers. So what?

'We're not teenagers, Jake,' she scoffed back, adopting the brittle taunting manner she always used with him, knowing it was her best form of protection. 'When Ralph and I want to indulge in passion we don't normally do so in the front seat of a parked car.'

'Perhaps not. But he didn't come in with you. He isn't staying the night.'

'Which is perhaps just as well,' Jamie told him in clipped accents. 'Why have you come here tonight, Jake?' she demanded curtly. 'It's no use blaming me because Amanda doesn't want to marry you.' She lifted her head and looked at him scornfully. 'She's not a fool, you know. She knew you weren't in love with her, that you were using her. Just as you once tried to use me.'

She saw his face contort as he took a step towards her. Trapped in the black glitter of his eyes it was too late to move away. His fingers locked round her arms, his chest expanding and contracting rapidly beneath the jacket of the formal business suit he wore.

'Don't try to push me too far, Jamie,' he warned her roughly. 'Sometimes you . . .'

The fierce surge of rage she could feel emanating from him excited her, shockingly so, her mind trying to ignore the signals coming from her body.

'Stop goading me,' he told her softly, giving her a little shake when she opened her mouth to deny his accusations, his fierce, 'Oh yes, you are, and you know you are, damn you,' suspending the words before they were uttered. 'One of these days you're going to push me further than you expect. And then what will you do? Cry rape?' he asked her brutally, watching the colour come and go in her face. 'But it wouldn't be rape, would it, Jamie? You want me, no matter how much you loathe admitting it. I could take you into your bedroom and make love to you now, and you know damned well that . . .'

'No!'

Her voice sounded unnaturally sharp and high, her face burned, shock fuelling her anger. How could he know the effect he had on her?

'What did Amanda say to you?'

His abrupt change of course shocked her. Amanda... That was why he had come to see her, because of Amanda.

'That you were pressuring her into marriage,' she told him flatly, rubbing her aching arms as he suddenly released her, the anger she had sensed in him earlier now transformed to sharp-eyed scrutiny. 'That between you, you and her father were putting her in a position where she'd have no alternative but to marry you.'

'Her father?'

Jamie was on safer ground now. 'Oh, come on,' she demanded scornfully. 'Don't tell me you didn't know that Amanda's father wanted her to marry you?'

'He had dropped the odd hint,' Jake agreed carelessly.

'And you suddenly realised that here was the ideal opportunity to provide Mark with a grandson, and at the same time secure your own inheritance.'

'Is that what you think? Amanda's an extremely attractive girl. I might have desired her for herself alone.'

Pain like a thousand knives tormented her flesh, but she shut it off, telling herself she mustn't let him get to her.

'It's what Amanda thought,' she countered curtly. 'She didn't seem to think that you cared anything for her at all.'

'And she came running to you.' His smile was a masterpiece of sardonic amusement. 'How you must have loved that, Jamie! Did you tell her, I wonder, how unaltruistic your championship was?'

'I told her nothing,' she came back sharply. 'And I certainly didn't encourage her, if that's what you mean, Jake.'

'No, but I'll bet you didn't give me any character references either, did you?' he asked softly. 'You're a very clever woman, Jamie. You've even managed to bring her father under your thumb. He tells me that he thinks Amanda is too young to be thinking of marriage. That's twice now you've deprived me of a bride, Jamie.' The glint in his eyes unnerved her.

'You could have married if you wanted to, Jake,' she told him breathlessly. 'Someone like Wanda.'

He shook his head, cutting her off urbanely. 'I think not. Wanda wouldn't have made good wife material.'

'Because you couldn't subject her to the same domination you could exert over an inexperienced teenager, is that what you mean? You've got an ego-problem, Jake,' she told him scornfully. 'Think about it. No real man needs to prove his maleness by dominating a child.'

'Careful, Jamie.' His voice was measured and uneven, but her ears caught the underlying anger. It gave her a fierce surge of pleasure to know that she had broken through his arrogant self-possession.

'Don't threaten me, Jake,' she told him contemptuously. 'I'm not eighteen any more.'

'So it would seem. Just how serious is this relationship with . . .'

'Ralph?' Jamie submitted mock-sweetly. 'What's the matter, Jake?' she taunted, suddenly filled with a surge of bitter-sweet pleasure. She wanted to hurt him as he had once hurt her, and yet perversely she longed to wipe out the past and the pain and to be once more the girl she had been when she thought he loved her. 'Frightened that I might after all be the first one to supply Mark with a grandchild?'

His whole face changed, the rage she could see clearly delineated in the look he gave her frightening her into silence. What had simply been a means of taunting him had suddenly become a dangerous weapon she was frightened to relinquish.

'You're going to marry him.' The words were harsh and sharp-edged, the effort of containing his fury compacting his face muscles. Her mouth had gone dry, apprehension flooding her stomach.

'Is there a law that says I can't?'

Such flippancy was insanity, but she didn't seem able to stop herself.

'You want to take it all, don't you, Jamie,' he said tightly, his voice menacing-soft as he told her, 'but I'm not going to let you.'

'What is it that makes you resent me so much?'

He came towards her and she lowered her lashes instinctively, but his fingers caught her chin, their pressure hard and determined as he forced it upwards until he could look into her eyes.

'Everyone thinks you're such an elegant, controlled lady, don't they?' he mocked softly. 'They should see you now, or better still, just after you've made love.'

'Love? Don't you mean sex?' Jamie spat at him, desperate to escape from his scrutiny. Every nerve-ending in her body was aware of him, and of the dangerous excitement kindled by their mutual anger. Even now, hating him for what he was doing to her, she ached for him, her body tense with the constraint she was putting on it.

'Call it what you like,' Jake told her tightly. 'Whatever name you give it, the reality was the same. Do you make those same sounds of pleasure for him that you made for me, Jamie?' he demanded softly, watching her.

It was impossible to breathe, her whole body was caught in the grip of a tension so encompassing that she couldn't move.

He was watching her, waiting for her to make a slip. Forcing herself to relax, she searched feverishly for the right flippant response. 'You mean you still remember?' she asked at last. 'You amaze me, I thought I'd have been forgotten long ago, buried deep beneath all those who followed me.'

'You're too modest.' His mouth curled unpleasantly. 'Much too modest.' His eyes were on her body and to her chagrin Jamie felt her nipples peak and harden beneath his glance. His hand moved and a wave of terror engulfed her. He mustn't touch her. Frantically she pulled away. 'I want you to leave, Jake.'

'I'm sure you do.' His smile was unkind but he did release her. 'Very well, I'll go, but don't forget the arrangements we made for Christmas, Jamie.'

'Christmas!' She jerked away from him, her eyes widening. 'I can't travel with you now.'

'Because Amanda won't be coming with us? Don't be ridiculous. Or were you thinking of taking the boyfriend home for parental approval?'

'Ralph? Of course not!' The moment the words were out she realised her mistake. He had given her the perfect excuse for refusing to go with him, and she had missed it.

The mocking triumph gleaming in his eyes warned her that he wasn't going to let her escape.

'And of course, you wouldn't dream of disappointing your mother and my father, would you?' he drawled softly. '*They're* looking forward to having you at home, Jamie. For their sake we ought to try and put on a happily united front, wouldn't you say?'

She opened her mouth to tell him exactly what she did want to say and then closed it again. How on earth had she ever been foolish enough to let him trap her into going home? But it was too late to back out now, and he knew it, damn him.

'You know, sometimes I almost forget you're not eighteen any more,' Jake taunted her softly as he stepped back from her.

'I'll see you to the door,' Jamie gritted in response.

He followed her without demur, halting only as she made to open the door. 'Just one more thing,' he drawled lightly.

'What?'

'This.' His arms came round her before she could move, imprisoning her against the heat of his body, so that any movement would only serve to bring her into even more intimate contact with him, his mouth finding hers with unerring accuracy.

She fought against response, refusing to give in to the clamour of her senses; to the drugging delight that spread through her veins, relaxing taut muscles.

It had been six years since he had last held her in his arms. Six years, but her body remembered the feel and taste of him as though it were yesterday.

Skilfully, determinedly, he drew from her the response she had fought against giving, and then just at the moment when her body started to relax against him, he released her, pushing her away.

Her first agonised feeling of loss was swiftly replaced by shock and rage as he smiled down at her, the expression in his eyes letting her know he was well aware of her arousal.

'Either he's a much worse lover than you deserve, or my performance was much better than I remember,' he mocked her softly. 'If I didn't have pressing business which takes me home, it might almost be worth while staying to discover which.'

She wanted to hit him, but his fingers seized her arm as she raised it, his voice cold as he warned,

'Don't do it. You won't like the way I retaliate. Hate me as much as you like, Jamie,' he told her as he left, 'but you can't deny that sexually I still excite you.'

She closed the door behind him and then leaned against it, willing her shaking body to relax. How could she have betrayed so much to him? How could she have been so stupid? She ought to have known how it would be. It was obvious that he was furiously, dangerously angry over Amanda's defection, and he had come round determined to take it out on her. And he had succeeded, she admitted wearily.

CHAPTER FIVE

'WISE girl. I'm glad that for once you've behaved sensibly.'

Resisting the temptation to hurl her case at him, Jamie let Jake take it from her and put it in the boot of his car which she now recognised as the expensive BMW that had been parked outside her house on the evening of the Johnsons' party.

She was sorely tempted to tell Jake that the reason she was going to Queensmeade with him had nothing to do with him personally, but she resisted it.

Right up until last night she had been determined that she would find a way of not going, and then yesterday everything had changed. Early in the evening her mother had telephoned to tell her how glad she was that she was coming home for Christmas. Her shaky, 'It might well be Mark's last,' had rocked Jamie's world to its foundations, and it had been several seconds before she had been able to find the breath to ask her mother just what she meant. It seemed that Mark's heart condition was far worse than had first been suspected and that his chances of living for more than a matter of months were very slim, but her mother's 'I'm so glad you're coming home, he's missed you, Jamie,' had banished for ever her thoughts of staying away.

'You mustn't mention his illness to him, though,' her mother had warned her. 'He hates anyone talking about it. He just wants to pretend that everything's... normal.'

Jamie could understand that and had had to swallow hard on the lump of pain forming in her throat. Mark might be Jake's father, but she loved him too. All at once she had been guiltily aware of how little she had seen of Mark and her mother since she left home. She would have gone back more, but Jake was always there.

'Going to stand there all night, are you?'

Compressing her mouth, she got into the car. She wasn't going to discuss her anguish over Mark with Jake. She could see nothing in his hard face to show that he was grieving over his father, but then why should he? She caught herself up, knowing she was being unfair. Jake loved Mark; she knew that.

'Mother says that Mark is much worse than they first thought.'

Jake turned to look at her as he started the car, his face grim. He looked older and tired, lines of strain she hadn't noticed before grooving his skin. Without Mark the full burden of Brierton Industries would fall on Jake's shoulders, and although technically he had been in charge for several years, she knew that he consulted Mark on many of his major decisions.

'Yes.' His voice was terse, warning her that she was trespassing, but something made her press him.

'Is there nothing that can be done, surgery, drugs?'

'There is a new drug, but as yet it's still in the testing stage. If he can survive another twelve months, then...'

'Can he survive twelve months, Jake?' she asked him, turning to look at him as he manoeuvred his car out into the traffic.

'Maybe—given the right sort of incentive.'

This time there was no mistaking the clipped curtness in his voice. Jake didn't want to talk to her about Mark.

'He's looking forward to seeing you.' His low-voiced comment caught her by surprise. She saw Jake's mouth curl in faint cynicism. 'Come on, Jamie. You know you always were his favourite.'

She couldn't deny it. Mark had always loved his son, but she had been the one he had spoiled.

'He's missed you.'

The quiet words made her feel unbearably guilty, but Jake was the one who should be feeling that, not her. Jake was the reason she had been forced to leave her home and stay away from it, Jake who had taken her foolish, silly dreams and smashed them on the hard cruelty of reality. She had left home because Jake had broken her heart; but she had not told him that. In her letter she had claimed that she was too young for marriage; that she wanted her freedom and the chance to pursue her own life unencumbered by a husband and children.

She certainly enjoyed what she did, and took pride in her part in building up their business, but she was honest enough to admit to herself that without Ralph to take charge of their financial planning she would have been quite content to work on a much smaller scale. Her career was something she could have fitted in quite easily with the responsibilities of a family and a home, and when she saw how happy Beth was she envied her most acutely.

If only she could have met someone to take Jake's place; someone to love and who loved her, she would have married most willingly. The sophisticated façade she cultivated was just that. She was too much her mother's daughter really to enjoy her solitary existence. It wasn't so much that she was lonely; more that she grieved over the waste of the potential she knew was within her to create a happy home.

She missed the wide open spaces of the Dales, the warmth of the people and going back would only reinforce her dissatisfaction. But what alternative was there? She could find enough work to keep her busy in Yorkshire, she knew that, but moving home meant moving back into Jake's orbit, and that was something she couldn't endure. She only had to see him to be consumed by a soul-destroying mix of contempt and despair; to ache for him in a way that shamed her self-respect and left her wishing she had never seen him with Wanda, never listened to the other woman's revelations. If she had married him . . .

Abruptly she stamped down on the thought. What was wrong with her? If she had married Jake, sooner or later she would have been disillusioned. It was stupid and irrational to keep on yearning for some make-believe dream that never really existed. The truth was that she still loved him, and that that love prevented her from committing herself to any other relationship.

'There's a flask and some sandwiches in the back. It will take us quite a while to get back, and I don't particularly want to stop unless you do.'

She shook her head, and then said abruptly, 'Why prolong the agony? The sooner we get there the happier I'll be.'

She caught the way Jake's mouth hardened as he looked away from her, and stifled a sigh. It was an automatic reaction for her to be prickly and defensive with him now, and it seemed impossible that once they had been so easy and natural with one another that she could spend hours in his company without needing to speak. Now just the sound of his voice making the most mundane comment was enough to prickle her skin into acute awareness.

'You never let up, do you? Which one of us are you trying to convince, Jamie, me or yourself?'

He was too acute, and she felt the nerves in her stomach clench in tension.

'No one likes being coerced into something they don't want to do, Jake,' she snapped back. 'Just because everyone else gives in to your damnable arrogance, that doesn't mean I'm going to join them.'

'Arrogant? Is that how you see me?'

They were on the outskirts of London now, heading for the motorway, and she felt him look at her, but refused to turn her head to meet his eyes.

'Isn't that the way you are?' she countered stiffly. It would have been more sensible to say nothing and ignore him. She didn't want to be drawn into an argument with him. As she knew to her cost, Jake was a past-master at manipulating the facts to his own advantage.

When he didn't reply she glanced across at him, conscious of the mocking look in his eyes as they flicked across her face.

'You used to like it,' he reminded her softly. 'You found it exciting that I was ... masterful.'

Jamie almost choked on the humiliated rage boiling up inside her. And the worst thing was that she couldn't deny what he had said. She had even used that exact word.

'No doubt at eighteen I did,' she retorted, swallowing down her anger and replacing it with carefully manufactured mockery. 'Fortunately since then I've learned better.'

'You mean you think you have,' Jake corrected urbanely. 'No woman ever respects or wants a man who lets her push him around, Jamie, and if you're honest you'll admit that that's true.'

Part of her mind acknowledged that he was right, but she was damned if she was going to tell him so.

'I believe in men and women being equal partners in their relationships,' she told him coolly. 'The macho image is out of date, Jake. The days are gone when a man could ride roughshod over a woman's thoughts and opinions, simply because he is a man.'

'I agree.' His ready acceptance of her criticism stunned her. 'But I still maintain that most women want a man who's prepared to show them that he is a man, if need be, a man they can rely on in a crisis.'

He was right, but she wasn't going to tell him as much. 'There's a difference between strength and arrogance, Jake,' was all she could think of to say, glad to see the motorway sliproad approaching, knowing that Jake would need to concentrate on his driving instead of scoring points off on her.

It was only as she settled back in her seat that she realised she had enjoyed crossing swords with him.

She looked at him covertly, aware of the confidence and sureness of his movements. Six years hadn't changed him physically at all. He still exhibited that strong sexual vigour she had been so attracted to at eighteen. He was dressed casually for the journey, a cream woollen shirt tucked into stone-washed jade-green jeans.

He braked unexpectedly and as the seat-belt tightened around her she put out her hand automatically to stop herself sliding forwards. The shock of finding the muscled tautness of his thigh beneath her fingers shivered through her and she withdrew instantly, but even in that short space of time her senses recorded the heat of his flesh beneath the fabric of his jeans, the solidity of bones and muscle.

'Sorry about that,' she apologised stiffly, 'I thought I was going to slide forward.'

She couldn't look at him. If she did he might read in her eyes all that she wanted to conceal from him. Touching him had unleashed too many memories, memories of the satin firmness of his skin, of the caresses he had enticed from her, of the pleasure he had given her and taught her to give him. The sensation of his flesh beneath her fingertips was so deeply patterned into her that without any conscious thought at all her mind was filled with mental images of him. Shockingly she was aware of how much she had wanted to go on touching him to rediscover the maleness of his body.

'Are you all right?' His voice was almost abrupt. 'You've gone as white as milk.'

'Shock.'

'Because you touched me accidentally?' Jake's voice was derisory. 'I don't buy that one, Jamie. You're not eighteen any more, and even when you were...' His voice dropped and all at once the atmosphere inside the car became unbearably tense.

'Not because I touched you,' she protested thickly. 'I meant it shocked me when you braked unexpectedly. One thing certainly hasn't changed, Jake, you still seem to think the whole world revolves around you.'

'*Your* world once did.'

The words fell into a thick, heavy silence, stunning her with their cruelty. She had no defence against them at all. What he had said was all too true.

'You're not a career-woman at heart, Jamie,' he added curtly. 'You need a husband, children.'

She opened her mouth to tell him that he was wrong, and realised she couldn't. 'Trust you to come up with something like that,' she said bitterly at last. 'No doubt you think a woman's place is in the home.'

'Not necessarily. Some women do need the challenge of a full-time career, others work because they have to for financial reasons. I'm not the chauvinist you seem to think, Jamie. I merely said that you weren't a dedicated career-woman. You worry too much,' he told her brutally, 'and it shows. You're nearly a stone underweight, you're tense and so brittly on edge you're in danger of falling apart.'

She was so taken aback that she couldn't find the words to formulate any defence. Worse, she knew that what he said was quite true. Apprehensive and shaken, she turned away from him, closing her eyes, letting the smooth motion of the car soothe and lull her.

It was the sudden sensation of losing speed that eventually woke her, her mind confused, and her body aching slightly as she opened her eyes to almost total blackness.

'Why have we stopped?'

Jake was unfastening his seat-belt, but when he reached across and flipped open hers she stiffened defensively.

'You're as wary as a stray cat,' he told her sardonically. 'I wonder why?'

'Where are we, Jake?'

'Only ten miles or so from home.'

'Then why have we stopped?'

'So that I can give you this.'

One hand curled round her left wrist, the other extracting a small box from his pocket. Her breath caught in her throat as he flipped it open and she saw the frosty glitter of diamonds. She recognised the ring immediately; they had chosen it together in York just before her eighteenth birthday.

Her eyes went from the ring to his face. Half in the shadow, it was impossible to read. A feverish tension gripped her, her body automatically straining away from him.

'Jake, what on earth do you think you're doing?'

Her flesh shrank beneath the coldness of the gold as he slid the ring on to her wedding-ring finger, her voice, which she had tried to make contemptuous and scornful, shamefully weak and quavery.

'Isn't it obvious?' He sounded mocking, his expression revealed to her as he moved his head slightly. The expression of hard determination in his eyes chilled her.

'Is this some sort of game?' Jamie moistened her lips, hardly daring to breathe.

'Not to me. My father's a sick man, Jamie,' he told her softly. 'He wants to see me married, he wants a grandchild. Thanks to you that's not now going to happen, is it?'

'You mean . . . you mean Amanda?' She felt frighteningly weak, her skin burning where his fingers still shackled her wrist, his thumb almost absently probing its fine veining and thudding pulse. For a moment the movement stopped. She saw him frown and look sharply at her.

'Amanda? Yes,' he agreed blandly. 'Twice now you've deprived me of my bride, Jamie. There isn't going to be a third time.'

It took several seconds for his words to sink in. When they did she stared at him in appalled silence before bursting out frantically, 'You can't mean you expect me to marry you?'

'Oh, but I can. My father's a dying man, Jamie,' he reminded her brutally, 'I can't afford to waste any time.'

'You're crazy!' She was actually stammering in her shock. Jake's mouth twisted slightly.

'I don't think your mother or Mark will think so.'

Her eyes searched his face, looking for some sign that this was all part of some silly, elaborate joke, but she could see nothing in his expression but hard determination.

'You can't make me,' she told him wildly. 'You can't make me do this, Jake.'

'Not by dragging you to the altar,' he agreed, 'but there are other ways.'

She knew then that he was going to touch her and shrank back from it, her body frozen with shock and fear. 'Why me?' she protested thickly as his hands gripped her shoulders and pulled her towards him.

'Because Mark loves you, because you're here, and because of this.'

His mouth moved savagely against hers, awakening a thousand memories she would rather have suppressed, his hands sliding down her back to pull her hard against his torso, his teeth tugging impatiently at her lower lip, demanding that she abandon herself to the eroticism of his touch.

When she kept her teeth firmly clamped together, fighting to resist her need to respond to him, his mouth left hers so abruptly she felt faintly sick with shock—and disappointment. His hands spanned her waist and shock exploded inside her when his fingers curled into the welt of her sweater and tugged it sharply upwards. By the time she had freed her arms to push him away it was too late, his fingers were cupping the satin-covered curve of her breast, easing away the fragile fabric of her bra.

Anger and desire fought inside her, a dangerous riptide of excitement threatening her self-control. She mustn't give in to him. She mustn't let him see how easily he could reduce her to aching desire. She managed to get one arm free and bunched her fist, swinging it wildly at his chest. His head bent towards her, his mouth unerringly finding the puckered outline of her nipple. The intimate contact of his mouth with her body unleashed a wave of almost pagan delight inside her. Her fingers uncurled unsteadily and pressed against his chest, the breath shuddering from her lungs. How many nights in the years they had been apart had she remembered him caressing her like this... No, not quite like this. Before he had always been gentle. Now he was not. Now there was a fine edge of violence to the way he touched her and shockingly her body seemed to respond to it, her nipple hardening eagerly in the heat of his mouth and thrusting against his tongue almost as though it sought its rough abrasion.

His fingers moved to her other breast, trembling slightly as they uncovered it, his mouth finding the frantic pulse thudding at the base of her throat.

'Nothing's changed, Jamie,' he whispered against her ear, 'I still want you and you want me.'

She opened her mouth to deny it and shuddered beneath the hot assault of his kiss. Dimly she was aware of him moving, and lifting her against him so that she was lying against his body. He had unfastened the buttons of his shirt and she felt the shudder tear through him as he pressed her breasts into the heat of his chest.

An unbearable ache exploded in the pit of her stomach, her body agonisingly aware of his arousal and her own desire to appease it. His hands moved down her back, pressing her tightly against him, his breathing laboured and harsh. His hand moved down the back of her thigh and then up again, his fingers spanning the rounded curve of her bottom.

His mouth left hers, his voice raw and unfamiliar against her ear. 'I want you, Jamie. Tell me you want me too.'

The past was forgotten, her body responding joyously and eagerly to his touch, the need he aroused within her now wholly adult.

'Jake...' His name left her throat on a long moan of surrender and supplication, her lips parting eagerly at the touch of his. All she could think of was how he was making her feel and the ultimate ecstasy of his full possession, and then incredibly he was setting her free, putting her back in her seat, and casually straightening her clothing.

'*Now* tell me you don't want to marry me,' he suggested softly.

She went red with the humiliation of it.

'You want me, Jamie, and I want you,' he told her when she said nothing. 'I could have taken you right here in the car and you wouldn't even have tried to stop me.'

'Just because I want you physically it doesn't mean I want to marry you, Jake,' she managed to say at last, hating the low rumble of laughter that moved his chest.

'Ah, but you see I'm the old-fashioned type,' he taunted her mockingly. 'The only way you're going to get my body is legally.'

How long had he known how vulnerable she was to him? Jamie wondered, agonised. And he *must* have known, otherwise he would never have touched her like that. It tore her apart that he was prepared to use her vulnerability against her so callously, simply substituting her for Amanda because he had decided he wanted a wife.

'You can't do this to me, Jake.'

The words spilled jerkily from her lips, misery welling up inside her. Marriage...marriage to Jake. After all these years it had come back to this. Full circle, so to speak. But more appalling than anything he had said to her, or done to her, was how she felt. She wanted to marry him, she acknowledged defeatedly, or at least a part of her did.

'I'm not doing it *to* you,' he told her curtly, 'I'm doing it *for* Mark. Try thinking of someone other than yourself for a change, Jamie. My father's a very sick man, and nothing will give him more pleasure than to know that we're getting married. It's what he's always wanted,' he added quietly.

Jamie shot him a venomous look. 'Which was why you proposed to me the first time round, no doubt!'

His eyelids lowered as though he wanted to hide his thoughts from her, a muscle beating briefly in his jaw.

'We haven't got time to argue about the past tonight, Jamie, much as you might enjoy doing so.'

'We *can't* get married.' She was whispering it now, knowing even as she made the denial that it had no substance.

'We *can* and we will.' Jake's words fell against her ears like chains, imprisoning her against her will.

Or was it? Didn't one part of her at least want to give in, want to be Jake's wife? The ambiguity of her own feelings appalled her. She looked at the ring glittering on her finger and moved it surreptitiously. It didn't move. It fitted too tightly for her to tug off. Panic welled up inside her. She heard the click of Jake's seat-belt and realised he was re-starting the car.

'You can't mean this!' She cried out the words despairingly.

'You know me better than that.'

'No one will believe we're in love. My mother...'

The look he gave her was unreadable, the dark eyes hooded, and although his voice was gentle when he said softly, 'Your mother isn't blind, Jamie,' the purpose behind the words was not.

'What do you mean?' She glared suspiciously at him, knowing she wasn't just fighting him, she was fighting herself as well. It would be so easy to give in, to tell herself that she had no choice, to let him marry her and then spend the rest of her life aching for his love. That was what she could not endure, she acknowledged, knowing she loved him whilst he did not love her. Every time he touched her she would be fighting against betraying her feelings and he *would* touch her. He had not lied when he said he wanted her. Sweat broke out on her skin; the temptation simply to reach out and take what was being offered was so great that she ached physically with the strain of suppressing it.

'Work it out for yourself.'

He sounded laconically unconcerned now, his attention all on the road and he turned the car. Feverishly Jamie tried to unravel what he meant. Was he suggesting that her mother had known about the crush she had had on him? That she had known how desperately in love with him she had been? Perhaps she had at that. Teenagers weren't very good at concealing their feelings, and certainly in the early days of their relationship she had been the one to do all the running, deliberately seeking out Jake's company, wearing her prettiest clothes, doing everything she could to make him see her as a desirable woman and not his little stepsister.

And it had worked, but in the years after she had run away she had come to see that all he had ever felt for her was desire. He had never actually loved her, but had simply seen in her the right material to create a malleable, adoring wife, and the opportunity to unite their separate inheritances from his father.

The car was moving faster now, and short of jumping out of it and running away from him she seemed to have

little choice other than to accept this farcical situation he
had thrust on her. He had been clever, she acknowledged bitterly, waiting until now to tell her. But he
couldn't force her to marry him, even if she let him get
away with this charade that they were engaged. Slowly
she started to relax. He had caught her off her guard, but
she would find a way out of the trap he had sprung. En-
gagements could, after all, always be broken. Thus re-
assured, she settled down into her seat, smoothing her
jumper, her fingers stilling as she suddenly remembered
the sensation of his mouth against her breast. Her
stomach cramped agonisingly as she fought to shut out
the memory.

'Only another five minutes or so now.' Jake's voice was
bland, but she was not deceived. What thoughts were
going through that Machiavellian brain?

Even in the dark the bends of the country road were
familiar, her body automatically tensing as Jake braked
for the entrance to the gates.

Mark had bought this house at the same time as he had
bought the factory just outside York, and it was the only
home Jamie had ever known. She had been too young
when her father died to remember anything of her life
before she and her mother came to live there. The house
was early Victorian and solidly comfortable rather than
elegant. Lights streamed from several windows as they
drove past the front door.

'I'll park the car at the back,' Jake told her. 'I won't be
using it again tonight.'

They went in through the kitchen door, Jamie leading, Jake following, his fingers closing firmly round her
wrist as they went inside. She had hoped he would stay

behind to get their cases, but guessed quite well why he had not.

Her mother, who had originally come to the house as cook-cum-housekeeper, still preferred to do her own housework and cooking, although she now had a daily cleaner from the village, and the warm spicy scents of the kitchen instantly transported Jamie back to her childhood.

Trays of mince pies lined the scrubbed wooden table, her mother turning from the oven to beam at both of them.

'Jamie, Jake! You're earlier than we expected.'

'Mark?' Her stepfather's name caught in Jamie's throat as she lifted anxious eyes to her mother's face.

'He's had a good day today,' her mother said gently. 'He's in the sitting-room waiting to see you both.' She looked down and caught the glitter of Jake's engagement ring, her hand lifting Jamie's into the light, her eyes questioning.

'I finally persuaded her.'

Jake was a born actor, Jamie reflected, listening to the ruefully self-mocking note in his voice as he answered her mother's unspoken question. 'I think I must have caught her in a weak moment.'

He talked as though his supposed feelings for her were an established fact, and that made her frown slightly, until her mother said breathlessly, 'Well, you said you had a surprise for us this Christmas, but I never guessed.'

'Didn't you?' Jamie watched her mother grin.

'Well, only sort of. Let's say we hoped, your father and I. He'll be so thrilled about this, Jake. When you hinted that you were thinking of getting engaged he was so pleased.'

What would her mother say if she knew that when Jake had hinted that he was getting engaged he had had a very different bride in mind?

'Go on through and tell him. I'll make some coffee.'

As soon as they stepped into the hall Jamie hissed bitterly, 'You never told me your father was expecting your engagement.'

'Didn't I? I meant to. Perhaps I got distracted.' The look in his eyes made her skin burn.

'That's why you forced this charade on me, isn't it?' she demanded. 'Because of *your* pride. Because you couldn't bear to admit you'd been turned down!' Every word she uttered seemed to increase the savage pain tearing at her, but she couldn't stop.

'I suppose it hasn't struck you that my actions could be relatively selfless, that I might just want to make my father happy? Yes, it's true that I hinted that this Christmas I would be getting engaged, but it isn't my pride I want to protect, Jamie, it's my father.'

Both of them had stopped, and were facing one another, speaking in fierce whispers.

'You're the one who cost me my bride after all, aren't you? So it's only fair that you should be the one to make restitution. I can't disappoint him, Jamie,' Jake told her quietly, his anger dying away as suddenly as it had been aroused. 'And a marriage between us needn't be such a bad thing, need it?'

For the space of a heartbeat she was transfixed by the look in his eyes. Was she imagining things, or was Jake actually looking pleadingly at her?

She swallowed nervously, wanting to reach out and touch him, suddenly unsure if she knew any more what she did want.

'Jake!'

The kitchen door opened and her mother came into the hall carrying a tray, her eyebrows lifting a little as she saw them.

'We *have* only just got engaged,' Jake told her with a grin.

Incredibly Jamie felt herself blushing, her anger re-ignited by the casual way Jake managed to behave.

Her mother opened the door to the sitting-room, and they followed her in. Mark was sitting in front of the fire, reading a paper. When he saw them his eyes lit up.

He had got a lot thinner, Jamie noticed achingly, and the joy in his face when he saw her overwhelmed her with guilt. Jake's hand lay against the small of her back, and although she knew he couldn't mean it that way, his touch was vaguely comforting.

'Well, now. This is a surprise!'

Mark's eyes went from Jamie's face to Jake's and back again.

'I've brought you an early Christmas present,' Jake told his father, propelling Jamie towards him.

'My stepdaughter?' The grey eyebrows lifted in a gesture very reminiscent of Jake.

Circling her waist with one arm, Jake shook his head. 'Your daughter-in-law-to-be—my wife.'

The delight that radiated from the worn, tired face reinforced everything Jake had already told her. Numbly Jamie listened to his teasing comments, forcing herself to

smile when appropriate, wondering if anyone else noticed how artificial her behaviour was.

'You won't be waiting long to get married.' It was a
statement and not a question. Panic leapt inside her, her
throat clogged with apprehension and pain.

'Not too long.' Jake sounded assured. 'We want the
ceremony to take place as soon as possible after Christmas, and then we'll go straight from here to Switzerland.'

Switzerland? Her brain seemed to have switched off
and then she remembered—how could she have forgotten—that Jake always spent three weeks or so skiing early
in the year.

Her mother had poured the coffee, and Jamie took the
cup she handed her, drinking the scalding liquid automatically. Mark was saying something about champagne.

'Jamie.'

She looked up to find her stepfather's eyes on her. 'I
know I don't have to tell you how happy this makes me,
my dear. It's what I've always longed for, you and Jake.'

He had grown frighteningly frail since the last time she
saw him and fear and love clutched painfully at her heart.
How could she tell him that it was all a sham, nothing
more than make-believe?

Across his bent head her eyes met Jake's, and she saw
the smile of triumph in his eyes as he read the capitu-
lation in hers.

CHAPTER SIX

THE rattle of crockery and the delicious smell of freshly-made coffee woke her the next morning. As she opened her eyes her mother was just depositing a daintily set tray on the cupboard beside her bed.

'Mum, you shouldn't,' she protested guiltily, sitting up. 'You're far to busy to pander to me.' She glanced at her watch, shocked to discover it was gone ten. How long had it been since she had slept so deeply or so well? Far from her subconscious plaguing her during the night about the situation she was in, it had been strangely silent.

'Nonsense! You deserve a little bit of spoiling. Besides, it isn't often I get the chance.'

Once again guilt stabbed her, her mother's words reminding her how infrequently she came home.

'How's Mark?' Jamie asked, changing the subject and sipping her coffee. It was delicious. No one made coffee quite as good as her mother's.

'Not too well, I'm afraid.' Her mother's face was unhappy. 'He's being so good, doing all that Dr Forster tells him, but . . .'

'Jake told me there's a possibility of a new drug.'

'Yes, but it could be twelve months at the earliest before it's available, although Dr Forster says the tests on it have proved very hopeful.' She reached out and touched Jamie's arm. 'I can't tell you what your news means to Mark, Jamie. He's always adored you. I sometimes think he married me more to get you as a daughter than me as a wife!' She smiled to show that her comment was only a joke, and then added more seriously, 'Hearing that you and Jake are to get married is just what he needed to make him cling that little bit harder to life. Some days he's in considerable pain, and it's that that Dr Forster worries about most. He can't give Mark anything to stop it, and I'm frightened that it might get too much for him. That he'll simply stop fighting.'

The tears in her mother's eyes shocked Jamie, bringing home to her the fact that she and Mark were not immortal. All through her growing years her mother had been the one she turned to for comfort and reassurance and now, too quickly, their rôles were being reversed. She touched her mother's bent head awkwardly, not knowing what to say. The usual words of reassurance would be meaningless in the circumstances.

'Silly of me to give way like that. It's just that your news couldn't have come at a better time. It's like the answer to a prayer. Of course Jake hinted some time ago when Mark was first ill that he was thinking of getting married, but we never dreamed... It's like a private dream come true for Mark, you know. He's always hoped that the two of you... I've got to go and see the vicar this afternoon—I'm organising the decorations for the Christmas Eve carol service. Jake suggested that you and he come with me so that you can talk over the details of the wedding ceremony with him. I gather that you both want something relatively quiet?'

What could she say? How could she destroy the hope and pleasure she saw shining in her mother's eyes? She looked back over the years and saw all those small unselfish acts that had been done for her, all the love and care she had received. Now it was her turn.

'What are you doing about a dress?'

'Nothing—yet. There hasn't been time.' That much was true at least. 'I thought I might find something suitable in York—a silk suit, though, rather than a dress.'

'Mmmm. We could spend the day there tomorrow. I had planned to go in anyway to do the last of my Christmas shopping. We're having our usual Boxing Day party, of course—it will make an ideal opportunity to announce your engagement—and the wedding. Will Beth and Richard be coming?'

Things were running away with her, Jamie thought helplessly, trying to stem her mother's eager flood of questions.

''We wanted you and Mark to be the first to know,' she said weakly. 'I'd like Beth to be there, of course.'

She looked up as her bedroom door opened, her eyes widening as Jake walked in. He was dressed formally in a dark suit. 'I'm just on my way to the factory,' he told them both. 'I thought I'd just pop in and say "good morning" before I left.'

Her mother rose with an indulgent smile, her eyes twinkling. 'Will three o'clock this afternoon suit you for seeing the vicar, Jake?'

'That's fine. I haven't any appointments, but there's some paperwork I want to clear away before the Christmas break. And that reminds me—it's the staff "do" tomorrow night They're holding it at the Post House—a dinner-dance. I forgot to mention it to you before, darling.' Jamie sucked in her breath indignantly at the casual endearment. 'We'll have to put in an appearance, of course.'

'I can't possibly go, Jake. I haven't brought anything suitable to wear.'

There was a moment's silence, and Jamie realised her mother was regarding her with a slight frown. Perhaps she had been over-vehement, but she was tired of Jake manipulating her.

'I'm sure we'll be able to find you something tomorrow, Jamie. You'll enjoy it, I know. Mark and I have always attended in the past, but this year...'

Watching the shadow darken her eyes, Jamie felt fresh remorse. 'Mark would like you both to go. The staff appreciate it so much, and it's become something of a tradition.'

Jamie knew when she was beaten. Swallowing down her ire, she shrugged her shoulders and said wryly, 'Well, it seems that I'm outvoted.' Her mother was already opening the door, and knowing that her temper would not stand any more clashes with Jake, she said pointedly to him, 'I won't keep you, *darling*, I'm sure you're anxious to get off.'

'Not as anxious as I am to wish my brand-new fiancée good morning.' His voice was as smooth as satin, the look in his eyes all that any newly engaged girl might hope for, but Jamie wasn't deceived. She barely waited for the door to close gently behind her mother before launching into her attack.

'I don't know what you're doing in here, Jake, but you can leave—right now,' she told him bitterly. 'Or are you just waiting to gloat over the way you've tricked and manoeuvred me?'

She saw his mouth thin as he walked over to the bed, and suddenly she wished she weren't lying there wearing only a brief satin nightshirt. The dark-suited male form leaning over her made her feel acutely vulnerable, and not just vulnerable, she acknowledged inwardly, feeling her nipples harden against the supple fabric. Half an inch of snowy white cuff protruded beneath the sleeve of Jake's jacket, his wrist sinewy and brown against the pristine fabric. He reached closer to her and she shivered involuntarily, her eyes transfixed, but instead of touching her he simply reached past her, picking up her coffee-cup and draining its contents.

'Umm, no one makes coffee like your mother's. I came in here simply because your mother would have been expecting me to,' he told her quietly, 'that's all.'

His quiet reasonableness deflated her, and for some reason she had an urge to annoy him, to make him react more positively. 'It's all right for you,' she told him bitterly, 'You aren't the one who's being forced into sacrificing his life. You...'

She gasped as his fingers gripped her shoulders, hauling her half out of the bed. Her toffee-coloured satin nightshirt clung to the curve of her breasts, but Jake apparently wasn't aware of that. He shook her—hard—his mouth a tight line of anger.

'Just when the hell are you going to grow up?' he demanded bitingly. 'Of course I'm making a sacrifice. Hasn't it struck you yet that I might not want this marriage any more than you do? If you hadn't meddled...'

'Meddled? I didn't meddle. Amanda came to see me, not the other way round. And if you don't want to marry me then what was all that about yesterday? You told me you wanted me,' she reminded him.

His mouth relaxed, curling into a mocking smile as he studied her flushed angry face.

'And so I do,' he drawled, 'but I don't have to marry you to satisfy *that* need.'

The sheer arrogance of his statement took her breath away, her eyes opening wide and then spitting fury at him as he laughed and then stroked a possessive hand down over her satin nightshirt, his fingers coming to rest over the rounded fullness of one breast, his thumb lazily teasing her quivering erect nipple.

'I could take you now,' he told her mockingly, 'and what's more I could make you enjoy every single second of it—and come back for more, but that's not why I'm marrying you.'

'No,' Jamie agreed bleakly, unaware of how much of her chagrin was showing in her face. 'You're marrying me because of Mark.' His eyelids had dropped, hiding his expression from her. 'Because he's your father, and you love him.' She was having difficulty in swallowing, suddenly, terribly aware of how little she had changed. She still wanted Jake's love. The bitterness of that knowledge overwhelmed her, filming her eyes with tears she was quick to blink away.

'Yes,' Jake agreed sombrely, releasing her and standing up. 'I'm marrying you because of love.'

She was completely trapped, Jamie acknowledged when he had gone, and not just by her love and loyalty to Mark. She wanted to be Jake's wife; she had always wanted to be his wife. But not like this, not without love. Six years ago she had run away from him vowing she would not marry someone who did not love her, but now here she was committed to that self-same marriage. Tears clogged her throat; her body ached with pain and misery. She was twenty-four years old, for heaven's sake— not eighteen; maybe the marriage was something she couldn't escape from, but surely betraying her feelings to Jake was?

'There's a little shop just along here where they might have something. I've never actually bought anything there myself, but I've often seen lovely things in the window. The girl who runs it designs a lot of the things herself. She specialises in bridal and formal gowns.'

Following her mother down one of York's quaintly narrow wynds, Jamie suppressed a sigh. Events were moving with a speed which she found frankly appalling, and even fate seemed to be conspiring against her. Only yesterday, right after they had got back from seeing the vicar, Beth had telephoned, and before Jamie could stop her, her mother had passed on to her their news.

Jamie had heard Beth's squeal of excitement right across the room. Of course her cousin had taken her to task for keeping her romance a secret, but that apparently was not going to stop Beth and Richard coming north for the wedding.

'What a pity Sarah isn't older,' Beth had moaned before she hung up. 'She could have made an adorable flower girl.'

'It isn't going to be that sort of wedding,' Jamie had told her firmly, ignoring Beth's anguished protests.

Now she gave her mother a slightly suspicious glance. 'I'm not looking for a traditional wedding dress, Mum,' she reminded her.

'Oh, I know that, dear, but there's no harm in seeing what Meredith has in stock, is there? And don't forget, you're going to need something for tonight's do as well.'

Jamie didn't want reminding. It irked her that she was going to have to attend the dinner-dance tonight, and she wasn't sure if, in her present fragile state of mind, she was up to playing the rôle of Jake's adoring fiancée.

Jamie left it to her mother to outline to Meredith what she wanted, and then wished she hadn't as the diminutive blonde smilingly produced several frothy confections in satin and lace.

'Mum, I don't want anything like that,' she reminded her parent. 'Besides, they're far too young for me.'

'Nonsense,' her mother told her firmly. 'You're twenty-four, for heaven's sake, that's all. I know how you feel, Jamie, I felt the same way myself, but I promise you later I regretted it.'

'These gowns will cost the earth,' Jamie protested when Meredith had turned away. 'I can't afford it, Mum.'

Smiling triumphantly, her mother announced, 'That's no problem. Mark wants to buy your wedding-dress.' She saw Jamie's face and said pleadingly, 'Please, darling, it means so much to him. You're as much his daughter as Jake is his son. You know that.'

'I know that if I were it would make this marriage incest,' Jamie grumbled, but she knew she was already weakening. She fingered one of the dresses gently. The cream silk billowed from the smallest waist imaginable, the lace and pearl-trimmed bodice vaguely Tudor in style.

'Try it on,' Meredith urged. 'It is actually the stock model I keep so that brides can get an idea of what they look like in it, but it's a small size, and if you wanted it I could do whatever alterations were necessary very quickly.'

It seemed the fates were conspiring against her, Jamie decided numbly, allowing herself to be coaxed and persuaded into the dress. Needless to say it fitted perfectly, confounding her own private belief that she could not possibly have such a tiny waist.

The look on her mother's face when she showed it to her killed any final thoughts she had of rebelling. Her mother wanted her to wear it, she realised wryly, and suddenly she didn't have the heart to disappoint her.

She had expected that after the wedding-dress finding something to wear for the dinner-dance would be something of an anti-climax, but she was proved wrong.

'I've got just the thing,' Meredith told her. 'Same size as the wedding-gown, so I know it will fit you. Just hang on a sec.'

She disappeared into the back of the shop and returned with the dress draped over her arm. Holding it up to invite her inspection, she asked Jamie, 'What do you think?'

The dress was a dense cobalt blue embroidered very strikingly in patterns of tiny black beads. It was cut along the lines of the exotic costumes worn by Latin-American dancers, although fortunately it was slightly more respectable.

When Jamie commented on this Meredith nodded her head. 'Yes, that's where I got the idea. Those dresses are so wonderfully sexy, aren't they?' She pulled a slight face.

'This doesn't go anywhere near as far as they do, of course, but I think it will create quite an impact.'

Fingering the supple material, Jamie shook her head. The mere thought of appearing in front of Jake in such a dress made her pulses throb, and that despite the fact that it possessed long sleeves and a demurely high neck. It didn't take a lot of imagination to picture how it would look, clinging to her body, and she suspected that it was designed to cling so tightly that it would be virtually impossible to wear anything other than the briefest underwear beneath it.

'It's lovely, but possibly a little too daring for the Works do.'

'Nonsense!'

Her mother's comment astounded her, and she looked rather doubtfully at her. 'It's a bit over the top, Mum.'

'Of course it isn't. If you wore it in London I doubt if anyone would raise so much as an eyebrow, and we aren't totally behind the times up here, you know. Go and try it on.'

Unwillingly Jamie did as instructed. She had to remove her bra, of course, and as she had expected the stretchy dress clung snugly to her body. While it covered every inch of her at the front the same couldn't be said for the back, she reflected wryly, studying her reflection in the mirrors. The scooped-out back dipped down almost to the base of her spine, the bias-cut handkerchief-pointed skirt swishing provocatively round her legs as she walked out of the cubicle to show the dress to her mother.

'See what I mean?'

'It looks stunning on you,' her mother pronounced firmly, her mouth relaxing into a smile as she teased, 'Are you worried that Jake might not approve? I know he's inclined to be jealous, Jamie, most men in love are, but I'm sure he'll also be very proud of you. Can't you see, he wants to show you off.'

Jamie opened her mouth to tell her mother just how wrong she was and then closed it quickly. It was too late to go back now. She was committed to this marriage whether she wanted it or not, and nothing could be achieved by telling her mother that far from loving her, in reality Jake merely wanted her.

'We'll take them both,' she heard her mother saying to Meredith as she walked back into the changing-cubicle.

They spent the rest of the afternoon in York, getting the last of her mother's Christmas shopping and visiting on her insistence a florists to arrange for flowers for the wedding.

'There really isn't any need for this fuss,' Jamie protested as they left the shop, but she knew she was wasting her time. Her mother was enjoying this, she acknowledged wryly, and why not? At least it might stop her worrying so much about Mark. It hadn't escaped her notice that her mother had aged recently; that there were new lines on her skin, and that she seemed to have lost some of her old vigour. Today that vigour had returned with a vengeance.

It was only as they were on the point of leaving that it struck Jamie that she would be expected to give Jake a Christmas present. Of course she had nothing for him. They were halfway back to the car when her mother stopped dead in her tracks and moaned.

'Oh no, I meant to call in at the hairdressers and fix an appointment for myself for the wedding. She closes tomorrow until after Christmas. I'd better nip back. Here,' she gave Jamie the car keys, 'you wait in the car for me.'

It ought to have been impossible to find a Christmas-cum-wedding present for a man one both loved and loathed in less than half an hour, but incredibly she found something almost straight away.

Two shops on from where her mother left her was a small jewellers specialising in hand-crafted items in gold and semi-precious stones. The moment she saw the dress cufflinks in the window, Jamie knew they were exactly what she wanted. There was no price on them, but studying the workmanship of the slightly rounded rectangles of polished stone in their surrounding of gold, she knew they were going to be expensive.

Two small diamonds set one either side in the gold added a raffish richness to the links. They were luxurious and unusual; and the stones were exactly the colour of Jake's eyes. They were the sort of gift a woman would only give to a very important man; or that a very sophisticated and very rich woman would buy for her lover, she acknowledged, a small smile curling her mouth. One thing was certain, no man would ever buy them for himself.

Before Jamie could change her mind she walked into the shop. They were as expensive as she had feared, but she knew she had to have them. Closing her eyes as she produced her credit card, she told herself it would be worth every penny just to see Jake's face when he unwrapped them.

Her mother and Mark would think them a gift from an adoring fiancée, but Jake would know better. He had said he wanted her, and the cufflinks said that she wanted him, and moreover that she was prepared to pay for that pleasure. He would be very angry, but it was high time he realised that he could not have everything his own way.

Jamie reached the car seconds before her mother and together they packed their parcels into the boot.

The temperature had dropped sharply during the day and now it was bitingly cold.

'I shouldn't be surprised if we had snow tonight,' her mother forecast as they drove home. 'I can smell it in the air.'

Mark said much the same thing as the three of them drank tea and toasted themselves in front of the fire, but if she had hoped that the threat of bad weather might make Jake change his mind about their going out, Jamie was disappointed. He came in just after six, shaking his head when her mother offered him a cup of tea.

'No time,' he told her, glancing at his watch. 'We'll have to leave at seven. I'd better go upstairs and shower. Of course I wouldn't say no to something a little stronger, brought to me by my lovely fiancée.'

He watched as Jamie coloured angrily beneath his apparent teasing. What was he trying to do? Persuade their parents that they were already lovers?

'Now, Jake, that's enough of that,' cautioned Mark. 'You're embarrassing the lass!'

Even though they were supposed to be engaged, her mother had not suggested that they might want to share a room. Their parents weren't old-fashioned, and perhaps if they hadn't been stepbrother and sister as well as an engaged couple, if Jake's fiancée had hitherto been a stranger to them, both Mark and her mother would have happily turned a blind eye to any covert sexual relationship prior to their marriage. Maybe her mother thought they were already lovers—it would be quite natural if they were had they really been in love—but she would not be happy about them pursuing the physical side of their relationship while they lived at home, and surely Jake must know that? Maybe he was just trying to get at her, and hadn't realised the interpretation their parents might put on his words.

'Jamie, I think you'd better go and get ready as well,' her mother cautioned her, breaking into her thoughts. 'Otherwise you'll be late.'

'Frightened?'

'Of you, or the evening ahead?' snapped Jamie, as Jake parked the car outside the hotel and switched off the lights.

She was actually feeling very nervous, but she refused to let Jake see it. As he opened the car door, his mouth compressing, she shivered in the intense cold, feeling her nipples hardening against the fabric of her dress. Jake had said nothing when she came downstairs, but she had been acutely conscious of his silent scrutiny and the way he studied her body.

'You should have brought a coat,' he chided her now, frowning as he locked the car. 'This isn't London, you know—it gets cold up here.'

'I was brought up here,' Jamie reminded him, clenching chattering teeth. 'But unfortunately I didn't realise I would be going out and I didn't bring a suitable coat.'

His mouth compressed again. 'Come on, then, we'll make a dash for it.'

Tiny flakes of snow were already covering the car park as he slid his arm behind her to support her. The sensation of the smooth fabric of his dinner-jacket against her bare skin was oddly erotic and this time when she shivered it had nothing to do with the cold.

She wanted to move away from him, but was all too aware that to do so would be to invite more scathing comments and so she let him hurry her inside the hotel in the shelter of his arm.

Perhaps because she had other things to worry her the evening wasn't the ordeal she had envisaged. In fact it was surprising to discover how many people remembered her, having known her as a teenager when she had often spent part of the summer holidays working in Mark's office.

They were a friendly crowd, ready to accept her both as her mother's daughter and as Jake's wife-to-be. She danced almost every dance, only one of them with Jake, and now as they were on the point of leaving she shivered slightly, remembering far too clearly the sensation of being held in his arms, his hand flat against her back, his fingers idly caressing the smooth curve of her spine.

He couldn't have been unaware of the way his touch made her react to him, her nipples hardening, her whole body going weak as he pressed her closer to him. Yes, he would have been as aware of her arousal as she had been of his, she reflected wryly, shivering as the hotel door opened and a flurry of snow whipped in.

'Looks bad out there,' one of the men commented. 'I don't envy you your drive home, young Jake.'

The car park was inches deep in snow and it was still falling. Gingerly Jamie stepped out, only to gasp in shock as Jake suddenly swept her into his arms, much to the amusement of the few guests who had not already left.

'I don't want my bride catching pneumonia,' he mocked for the benefit of their audience, but he didn't put her down until he reached the car and even then he did so slowly, taking obvious pleasure in the way her body slid helplessly against his.

'Stop it, Jake,' she warned him breathlessly as his body pressed her against the bulk of the car. 'I don't want this.'

'Liar!'

Nevertheless he did move away to unlock the car door, and not for the world was Jamie ready to admit even to herself that her body missed the heat and maleness of his, and that he was quite right to call her a liar.

As he manoeuvred the car out of the car park Jamie took time to be thankful that she *was* with Jake. There was no one else she would have trusted to drive her in such weather, but even so she didn't risk distracting him by making conversation, instead peering anxiously through the ever-thickening snow.

'Perhaps we should have stayed at the hotel,' she murmured hesitantly at one point when they turned off the main road, and she felt the tyres slide in the snow.

'I tried, but they only had one room,' Jake told her laconically. He watched her for a second, his mouth curling into a smile, his voice soft as he drawled, 'Disappointed?'

It was almost as though he had known about the erotic images rioting through her mind, Jamie thought tensely, squashing down the ache inside her. How could he really want her when he had just turned down an ideal excuse to have her to himself for the night?

'Several of our fellow guests were already booked in, and I thought if you and I stayed, sharing a room, it would only lead to gossip. This isn't London, you know,' he added tauntingly. 'In these parts certain standards of behaviour are expected.'

'That didn't stop you before.' The moment the words were out she stiffened. Why on earth had she said that?

'It might not have stopped me from making love to you,' Jake told her in a grating voice. 'But I don't remember ever subjecting you to the sort of gossip that follows an open and overnight stay at a very public hotel.' He laughed harshly, his voice hard as he added, 'You must have got me confused with one of your other lovers. I hope they were properly appreciative of all that I taught you.'

If he hadn't been driving she would have hit him, as it was she had to compress her anger deep inside as she tried to ignore the aching pain that went with it. Was that how he saw her, as a woman who went carelessly from one man's bed to the next? Was what they had once shared so unimportant to him that he didn't *know* that to her . . .

'That's it, I'm afraid. The car won't get any further down here.'

His abrupt announcement cut across her thoughts. The car had stopped without her realising it, and peering through the window Jamie realised they were halfway down the narrow lane that led to the house.

'The wheels are too firmly embedded in the snow for me to risk going any further. We could easily skid and hit the wall. We'll have to walk the last half-mile.'

Walk? Jamie stared at him and swallowed, thinking of her fragile high heels and her bare coatless back.

'I've got a sheepskin in the back that you can wear,' he told her abruptly. 'Come on, the sooner we get going the faster we'll be there. When we came out I hadn't bargained for it snowing as heavily as this.'

He reached into the back seat of the car and handed her a heavy sheepskin jacket. She pulled it on, huddling into its warmth and grimacing at the length of the sleeves, but at least it would keep her warm and fairly dry. Knowing that her high heels would be worse than useless, she slipped them off before getting out of the car. It would be easier to walk in her stockinged feet.

Jake was too busy locking up the car to see what she was doing and by the time he joined her she had already walked several yards.

At first it wasn't too bad. It was still snowing and the sharp icy flakes stung her skin and soaked her hair, but the sheepskin was warm and as long as she didn't think about her feet they didn't bother her.

It wasn't until they had almost reached the gates to the drive that she realised ominously that she couldn't feel them any more. Jake had had to slow down to match his pace to hers and now he turned to watch her as she took a fateful unwary step and felt the ground slide away beneath her.

She fell forwards, the snow cushioning her, but the impact still something of a shock. Her exhausted cold body didn't want to move and she closed her eyes on a deep shiver, wanting to stay exactly where she was. But Jake wouldn't let her, he was hauling her out of the snowdrift, cursing angrily as he brushed the snow off her.

'What the...?'

Numbly Jamie looked at him. He was staring in incredulous fury at her bare feet.

'I only had my high heels,' she mumbled nervously. 'I...'

'Are you crazy? You...' She saw him shake his head and then he lifted her into his arms, despite her protests that she could walk.

'Walk? Oh, you'd rather crawl there on your hands and knees than let me help you, I know that. You little fool! You could have got frostbite.' She felt his heart thudding against his ribs, his voice suspended as he fought against his anger.

'Frostbite? Isn't that a bit excessive?' She could afford to be more sanguine now; indeed she felt almost light-headed with the deliciousness of the warmth of his body against hers, and although a tiny voice told her that she should insist on walking home under her own steam, it was far too pleasant being held close to Jake like this for her to voice such an objection.

The snowflakes were drifting down slowly now, and she raised her hand to brush them off Jake's face. She never wanted the drive to come to an end. She wanted to stay here like this for ever... Jake blinked and snowflakes stuck to his lashes. Jamie touched them with her tongue, feeling them melt. Beneath her tongue his skin was cold.

'Jamie, what the hell do you think you're doing? Are you drunk?'

The harshness of Jake's voice shocked her back to reality. Was she drunk? She thought musingly for a while and then decided that no, she wasn't. She had only had three glasses of wine. But she was in the most delicious state of euphoria.

'I'm not drunk,' she told him solemnly, shivering suddenly as he put her down and she realised they had reached the house. 'But I am cold,' she protested in a small voice. 'Very cold.' And she was. Terrible shudders racked her body now that she was away from Jake's warmth.

She was barely aware of him opening the door, and snapping on the light. Of course her mother and Mark would be in bed. They never kept late hours. Jake closed the front door and bent purposefully towards her, picking her up again and heading for the stairs.

'Stay there,' he told her as he dropped her down on to her own bed. 'I'm going to get you something to drink.'

She was terribly cold. No, not just cold, she was freezing, Jamie acknowledged, shivering convulsively. What she wanted was a hot bath, the hotter the better.

Staggering towards her bathroom, she ran the water, tugging at her dress with almost numb fingers as the bathroom filled with steam.

'Jamie!'

The sound of Jake's voice shocked her. She had forgotten that he had said he would come back. It was too late to tug her dress back on, but even so she made a frantic dive for it as he thrust open the bathroom door.

'What the hell are you doing?'

'Having a bath,' she told him with angry dignity. 'What does it look like I'm doing?'

Incredibly he didn't make a move to leave her, saying bitingly instead, 'Well, get on with it then. Get in.'

Get in? With him standing there? 'What...?'

She gasped her shock out loud as he picked her up, swiftly divesting her of both tights and panties, before almost dumping her down in the hot water.

'I want you to go away,' she protested angrily, furiously embarrassed by his behaviour.

'No way. The state you're in at the moment if I turn my back on you, you're all too likely to drown.'

'It sounds like a good idea,' Jamie told him sarcastically. 'At least then I wouldn't have to marry you. Jake...Jake, what are you doing?' Her voice trembled betrayingly as he thrust off his jacket and rolled up the sleeves of his shirt. His arms were muscular and faintly tanned, just the sight of them enough to arouse the most dismaying sensations in the pit of her stomach. He grabbed her sponge before she could stop him bending over the bath to circle her ankle with one hand while the other applied the sponge vigorously to her foot. The sensation of feeling returning to her cold foot was agonising; but she bit back her sharp cry of distress, closing her eyes against the tears of pain clogging her throat.

'Serves you right for being stupid enough to walk through six inches of snow with nothing on your feet in the first place,' Jake told her with a grim lack of sympathy.

She glared at him, the pins and needles forgotten. 'And whose fault was that? I wasn't the one who turned down a perfectly good hotel room and got the car stuck in a snowdrift.'

'No, you weren't, were you?'

The soft silkiness of his voice unnerved her. In the heat of their argument she had forgotten that she was completely naked, but now suddenly she remembered it, a betraying blush spreading up over her skin.

'Interesting,' Jake commented laconically, studying the way her skin changed colour with cool scrutiny. 'I didn't think women of your age and experience did things like that. And as for the hotel room,' he continued blandly, ignoring the fulminating glare she was giving him, 'if that's what's making you so cranky...'

She squeaked in protest as he lifted her out of the bath, demanding breathlessly that he put her down and at the same time clutching on to his shoulders in case she accidentally slipped.

'Your voice tells me one thing,' Jake mocked her as he carried her back into her bedroom, 'but your body tells me another.'

His mockery brought her back to reality, her body recoiling from him as he dropped her on to her bed.

'Okay, you've had your fun, Jake,' she told him curtly, 'but now it's over. Please go away.'

'Not until I'm satisfied that you're not still half frozen and in danger of suffering from frostbite.'

He was smiling as he said it, but the gleam in his eyes alarmed her. 'I'm perfectly all right now,' she told him firmly, and then spoiled the cool effect of her words by starting to shiver.

'Here, drink this.' He handed her the glass of brandy he must have brought upstairs with him, standing over her whilst she drank it with a shudder of distaste. The glass empty she turned to put it on the bedside table. As she moved, the lamp illuminated the rounded curve of her breast, gilding her skin.

'There, it's all gone now, Jake,' she started to say as she turned back to him, but the words died as she saw the way he was looking at her.

'Jake?'

Her throat felt dry, aching with tension, her body trapped in the fierce beam of Jake's eyes. She wanted to hide herself away from him and yet conversely she was aware of a febrile excitement building up inside her as she saw the way he was looking at her.

'Jake.'

It was more of a plea than a reprimand, she recognised shakily, quivering responsively at Jake's hoarse,

'I'd forgotten just how feminine you were.'

He reached out towards her, his fingertips just brushing the round smoothness of her breast. She could quite easily have moved away, but for some reason she chose not to.

For some reason? Who was she deceiving? she asked herself achingly. She wanted this, had wanted it for so long that that wanting had become a part of her. Almost as though it were happening to someone else and not herself she was aware of the way her nipples hardened in excitement; of the dull ache coiling unrelentingly through her stomach.

Jake's shirt was wet where he had lifted her out of the bath, and now silently she leaned towards him, her fingers trembling over the buttons, no words necessary between them as he shrugged out of his unfastened shirt and held her against his body.

The sensation of his hard chest against her breasts was a pleasurable form of torment, the way he said her name before his mouth covered hers causing a shivering fever of need to race along her spine.

Endless moments passed while his hands and mouth caressed her into a state of mindless languor.

'Jamie.' Her name was a soft sigh against her skin before his lips tormented the vulnerable arch of her throat. Her head tipped back under the assault, her body quivering with an intensity of arousal she made no attempt to hide.

She felt Jake's fingers touch her skin, stroking down from her throat to her breastbone, while his teeth tugged delicately against the lobe of her ear.

With circles as light as a breath he traced the shape of her breasts, his touch so light and delicate that it was a form of torture. She must have made a sound of protest, betrayed something of her frustration, because she felt the way his chest compressed under the sharp breath he drew and then his mouth was against her breast, his tongue stroking the aching peaks of her nipples as he muttered between caresses,

'Is this what you want, Jamie? Is it?'

Her answer was a low moan of surrender deep in her throat, her fingers sliding into his hair, holding him against her body as she gave herself up to the sharp pangs of pleasure his mouth invoked. When his hands slid down over her skin and he pushed her back against the bed she made no attempt to stop him, protesting only briefly when his mouth left her breasts.

'Jake . . .' she protested feverishly as she felt him move away from her.

'Shush. It's all right.' He was standing beside her bed, tugging off his trousers. His body had once been as familiar to her as her own, but now the sight of it made her catch her breath in aching wanting. Without waiting for him to come back to her she moved towards him, her starved senses absorbing the male reality of him.

'Jake.'

She saw that he had read the message of wanting in her voice, and there was certainly no mistaking his own state of arousal. Her body ached for his possession. She reached out to touch him, stunned when he suddenly grasped her wrist, and moved abruptly away from her.

Rejection drove cruel spikes of pain into her heart, but Jake seemed barely aware of her, as he hurriedly pulled on his trousers and then his shirt, swiftly buttoning it and tucking it back inside his trousers.

'Quick, get into bed,' he told her harshly, flipping back the bedclothes when she didn't move.

'Jamie.'

As he spoke she heard a brief knock on her bedroom door, and then it opened. When her mother came into the room, Jamie was lying beneath the bedclothes, while Jake stood over her, holding the empty brandy glass.

'Jake?'

It was typical that her mother should look to Jake for an explanation rather than her, Jamie thought wryly.

'Don't get in a panic. We had a problem on the way home. The car got stuck in a snowdrift and we had to walk. Only your daughter decided not to bother wearing any shoes, so I made her come upstairs straight away and jump into a hot bath. I've just brought her a glass of brandy. I think she's okay now.' He looked questioningly at Jamie, and she nodded her head weakly.

'I was just going down to make a cup of tea. I couldn't sleep and I saw your light on. Are you sure you're all right, Jamie?'

'Fine, thanks to Jake's prompt doctoring.' Jamie hoped that she sounded more relaxed than she felt. It was ridiculous that she and Jake were reacting like a couple of guilty schoolchildren. But it wasn't for his own sake that he was doing it, she recognised. It was for her mother's. Privately she doubted that Jake would have given a damn about being found on the verge of making love to her otherwise.

'Well, if you're sure you're okay.' Her mother was moving back towards the door, and Jake was following her.

'I'm fine,' Jamie assured her again.

'I think I'm suffering more than the patient,' Jake commented drily as he opened the door for her mother and followed her through it.

Jamie had had time to slip out of bed and put on her nightdress before she heard the second knock on her door.

'I've brought you a cup of tea,' her mother announced as she walked in and put the mug down beside the bed. 'Jake's gone to bed. I'm glad to see you've put on your nightdress,' she added wryly. 'It will help to keep you warm. I do know what loving someone's all about, Jamie,' she commented, smiling at her. 'After all, Jake is very much his father's son.'

Was her mother hinting that she hadn't been deceived by Jake's story? Jamie suspected she knew exactly what she had interrupted. If she had thought that she might be able to find a way out of marrying Jake, she knew now that she couldn't. Now that her mother thought they were lovers, she would have to go through with it. There was no escape.

CHAPTER SEVEN

'Oh Jake, it's lovely! Where on earth did you find it?'

They were all unwrapping their presents, and Jamie peered over her mother's shoulder to admire the delicate miniature Jake had given her. Her mother collected them, but this one was particularly exquisite.

'I saw it in an antique shop in Bond Street,' Jake told her, smiling at her. 'I'm glad you like it.'

'Like it!'

Watching her mother hug him, Jamie suddenly felt left out, excluded almost. She had already unwrapped Jake's present to her, very quietly while no one was watching, and was guiltily aware that it was both carefully chosen and expensive. Against it she suspected that her gift to him would look very brash.

She was in fact already wearing it, having slipped out to put it on while the others were talking, and she touched it now, feeling the smooth metal that lay against her throat with fingertips that shook slightly.

Across her mother's bent head she felt Jake watching her. The cost of his gift to her on its own was nothing, but its beauty, the care that had gone into choosing it, those both disturbed her. The necklace, designed in the form of a rigid collar, narrow at the back and wider at the front, was fashioned from a smoothly beaten dull gold that complemented her skin, its surface set with seed pearls and turquoise.

119

She knew it was antique and guessed it had probably been made during the early nineteenth century when the passion for anything and everything Egyptian was at its peak.

Whatever its pedigree, the necklace was undoubtedly a beautiful piece of work, exquisitely detailed and extremely unusual, just the sort of thing she might have bought for herself could she have afforded it. In fact it was exactly the sort of present that only someone who knew her tastes very well could have chosen for her.

'You haven't unwrapped Jamie's present yet,' Mark reminded his son.

Looking away from her, Jake drawled, 'I'm saving the best for last.'

Across the space that divided them Jake looked at her again and smiled. She wished she had a tenth of his acting ability, Jamie thought miserably. It was becoming increasingly hard for her to maintain this fiction of being a happy bride-to-be. And added to that she was tormented by the memory of the ridiculously stupid way she had reacted to him the night of the dinner-dance. God, if she had worn a placard with the message written in foot-high letters, she could scarcely have made her feelings plainer! She tried to blame the wine she had had to drink, but she knew it was only an excuse. She had wanted him so badly that she simply hadn't been able to stop herself from responding to him. How long would it be before he guessed that she felt much, much more than mere physical desire for him?

The other three had gone quiet and she frowned, looking at Jake. He had unwrapped her gift and was studying the cufflinks.

'It's the "in" thing for a woman to buy the man she loves diamonds,' Jamie explained a little uncertainly to Mark and her mother, but she knew that Jake wasn't deceived.

He proved it to her later in the day when he caught her alone in the hall.

'I haven't thanked you yet for your present,' he told her silkily. 'Do you want payment in cash or in kind?'

'Neither,' Jamie told him flippantly. 'Consider them settlement for what I've already received.'

'Are you this generous to all your lovers?'

The drawled words stung, although she knew that she deserved them. 'That sort of generosity isn't necessary where they're concerned,' she came back dulcetly. 'After all, *they're* receiving the benefit of your expert tuition.'

She saw by the look in his eyes that she had gone too far, but before he could retaliate her mother walked into the hall, giving her the opportunity to escape.

Because of Mark's heart condition, they had a fairly quiet Christmas with only the family's closest friends at their Boxing Day cocktail party. All of them professed themselves thrilled over the engagement and Jamie was subjected to a good deal of good-natured teasing. Jake, she noticed, managed to remain aloof from all the teasing camaraderie, but then Jake could be extremely remote when he chose. As their eyes clashed she knew there was still a reckoning to come for her comments on Christmas Day, and she shivered, cursing her own hot-tempered impulsiveness.

* * *

The day of their wedding came round all too quickly. Beth and Richard drove up the evening before, arriving just before dinner. As she watched the look on Mark's face as Richard cuddled his sleeping daughter, Jamie knew that Jake had been right when he claimed that his father was longing for a grandchild.

'Come up and help me put your goddaughter to bed,' ordered Beth, taking the sleeping baby from her husband as she spoke to Jamie.

It was as good an excuse as any to escape from Jake's presence. With everything arranged for tomorrow's wedding, Jamie felt that her nerves were stretched to breaking point. So acutely attuned to Jake's presence had she become that she knew when he was in the room simply by the way her muscles tensed. If she felt like this in the comparative safety of her parents' home, how on earth was she going to react when she was actually alone with him? The mere fact that she chose to close her mind against such thoughts showed her how very vulnerable she was.

'Well, well, aren't you the dark horse,' Beth teased as she put Sarah down on the bed and started to undress her. 'Mind you,' she added complacently, deftly removing Sarah's nappy and laughing as the baby kicked happily, 'I never did buy that tale you tried to spin me. I always suspected there was far more to your relationship with Jake than you were letting on. Watch her, will you, while I go and get her bath?'

Obligingly Jamie knelt down beside the gurgling baby, tickling her plump stomach while Beth disappeared into the guest-room bathroom.

'Mind you, you are getting married in something of a rush,' Beth added teasingly a little later, when Sarah had been bathed and dried.

'Jake's concerned about Mark,' Jamie told her flatly. 'He isn't at all well.'

Instantly Beth's expression changed. 'Oh love, I'm sorry!' she commiserated, putting her hand on Jamie's rigid arm. 'I know how much you love Mark. I'm sorry if I was tactless. Of course Jake would want to give Mark the pleasure of seeing you married before...'

'It isn't as bad as that, Beth,' Jamie interrupted, seeing that her cousin looked very shaken. 'Mark *is* very ill, but there is a chance if he can struggle through a few more months that a new drug that's coming on the market will help him. We're both keeping our fingers crossed.' She bent down to pick up her goddaughter.

'We can pop her in her cot now,' Beth told her. 'She'll be asleep in no time at all. Where's Jake taking you on honeymoon?' she asked, checking that the baby was comfortable, before opening the bedroom door and snapping off the light.

'Switzerland,' Jamie told her. 'He normally spends three weeks or so there at this time of year, skiing. He always goes to the same resort. It's run by a French couple. There's a hotel, and a dozen or so separate chalets.'

'Umm, this year I don't suppose he'll spend much time skiing,' teased Beth, watching the colour come and go in her cousin's face.

Jamie was glad that Mark's illness meant that the evening came to an early close. Beth seemed to take it for granted that she and Jake were madly in love, and the strain of maintaining this pretence in front of yet more people was almost more than she could bear.

No one seemed to take it amiss when she excused herself shortly after her mother and Mark had gone to bed.

When Jake accompanied her to the door, opening it for her and then following her into the hall, she tensed automatically, turning on him just as the door was closed on Beth and Richard.

'You don't have to behave like my gaoler, Jake,' she told him angrily. 'I'm not going to make a bid for freedom.'

Something alien and almost frightening flickered in his eyes as he looked down at her. His voice was curtly harsh as he said bitingly, 'We're supposed to be very much in love—and on the verge of marriage. Beth and Richard would have thought it a little odd to say the least if I hadn't followed you. No doubt they think that right now we're both snugly ensconced in your bedroom enjoying a small illicit taste of the pleasure that will be legally ours tomorrow.'

Jamie felt her skin crawl with embarrassed colour. He was right, of course. Beth was both modern and thoroughly outspoken. She and Richard had been lovers before their marriage, and Jamie had no doubt that Beth took it for granted that the same applied to Jake and herself.

'I'm very tired, Jake,' she told him unevenly. 'And right now I'm not in the mood for arguing with you. After all, from tomorrow we'll have the rest of our lives to do that, won't we?'

She left him before he could say anything, almost running up the stairs in her haste to escape.

Once in her bedroom she was alarmed to discover that she was trembling. She paced her bedroom floor angrily for several minutes, wondering what it was about Jake that made her react like an idiotic teenager. At eighteen she hadn't behaved as stupidly as this... but then at eighteen she had believed that he loved her as much as she loved him. Her verbal defiance; her desire to lash out and provoke him sprang from fear, she acknowledged, ceasing her pacing to sit down on her bed. And that fear was that Jake might discover how she felt about him. She couldn't endure the humiliation of his discovering how vulnerable she was to him.

She got up tiredly, walking towards her bathroom, her body tensing as someone opened her bedroom door.

She knew before he walked in that it was Jake. That sensitive inner radar that operated so disturbingly where he was concerned had already relayed the knowledge to her.

He closed the door quietly behind him, leaning against it for a second as she stared at him in dry-mouthed apprehension. He looked completely relaxed and at ease, leaning indolently there, but when he moved it was with a fierce inner tension; an aura of coiled dangerous vibrancy.

'Jake!'

'It's all right, I haven't come here to fight,' he mocked, anticipating her. Instead of reassuring her, his soft words heightened her sense of fear. Backing away from him, she said wildly,

'Then what have you come for? I'm not going to let you touch me, Jake,' she warned him.

'It's all right—don't panic. Not that I don't want to. Perhaps it would do us both good,' he added half under his breath. As he saw the expression of bitter distaste flood her face, he smiled without humour.

'Come on, Jamie,' he demanded softly. 'You're a woman now, not a child. A woman with a beautiful body that's no doubt received its share of sexual homage. Physical frustration isn't easy to endure, but it won't be for much longer.' His eyes dropped to her breasts and infuriatingly Jamie felt them swell and start to ache in anticipation of a far more physical caress.

She started to tremble, all her anger and pain welling up inside her. 'Get out!' she snapped at him furiously. 'You might have forced me into this marriage, Jake, but you'll never force me into your bed!'

She saw the lazy good humour fade from his eyes, his mouth hardening as he drawled cruelly,

'What makes you think I'll need to use force? But have it your way if that's what you want, Jamie,' he added with a shrug. 'I came in here hoping we might be able to get things on a better footing, but it seems I was wrong. Until tomorrow, my wife-to-be,' he mocked softly as he turned towards the door.

Long, long after he had gone Jamie lay tense and awake, telling herself that she would never, never submit to physically becoming his wife, and yet knowing even as she made the bitter claim that should he choose to do so, there was very little he could not take from her. After all, he had already taken the most important thing. She had given him her heart six years ago; he held it still, and always would.

*   *   *

Jamie had often heard that it was quite common for brides to go through the day of their wedding without being able to remember a thing about it later, and certainly that was true of her.

Reality broke through her tense self-control only briefly when Mark walked her down the aisle to where Jake waited for her. Just for a brief moment she wanted to turn and run, and then almost as though he knew what she was thinking Mark whispered emotionally,

'Jamie, you don't know what this means to me, to see you and Jake married. It's what I've always wanted, for both of you, although I never expected the pair of you would make me wait this long,' he added with a wry chuckle.

And then it was too late. She was at Jake's side, and the vicar had begun the service.

It was just before she left the reception to change to her going-away clothes that Jake caught her alone, murmuring dulcetly against her ear,

'You make a breathtakingly beautiful bride, Mrs Brierton, although I must admit the white dress was rather unexpected.'

The cruelty of his jibe grated against her over-sensitive nerves, her voice unusually husky as she snapped back,

'You were the one who had my virginity, Jake.'

'True, but there have been plenty of others since me, although actually it was not your lack of virginal innocence that prompted my remark—I doubt many brides can lay claim to that, these days. It was simply the fact that you decided to dress as a traditional bride. I expected something far more severe and in keeping with that glossy career-woman image you project so well these days.'

'Mother wanted me to have it,' Jamie told him. 'She…'

'Sorry to come between you, but it's time Jamie got changed,' announced Beth, adding with a grin as she looked at Jake,

'Let me put it this way. The sooner she gets changed and the pair of you get on that plane, the sooner you'll have her all to yourself, Jake.'

'Umm, well, in that case I suppose I'd better let you take her away.'

How easily Jake assumed his self-imposed role, Jamie reflected as she allowed Beth to lead her away. She still felt as though she had strayed into an unending nightmare, from which her only solace was that she knew she must eventually wake up.

Beth chattered gaily while she helped her to change, and Jamie assumed she must have made the right responses. Her cases were already packed with the skiing clothes she had left behind when she went to London. They would still fit, although they were no longer fashionable, but what did that matter? While another bride might have wanted to dress to catch the eye of her new husband Jamie knew that Jake couldn't care less what she wore.

She had chosen her travelling clothes for comfort rather than elegance, but the close-fitting jade-green stretch-cord pants emphasised the slender length of her legs, the thick green and white patterned jumper she wore over the top casual and warm. Soft leather ankle-boots in the same jade as her pants completed her outfit, but Jamie gave herself no more than a brief cursory look as she pulled a brush through her hair and renewed her lipstick.

There was a brief knock on her bedroom door.

'That will be Jake,' Beth announced. 'I'll go and warn the others that you're ready to leave.'

The door opened and Jake walked in carrying a large cardboard box. Like her he was dressed casually in cords and a soft-checked shirt, a leather blouson jacket in the same dark green as his jeans held casually in one hand.

'I'll go and tell everyone you're on your way,' Beth told him as she sped through the open door. 'Don't be too long, though,' she warned him with a grin. 'We don't want you to miss that plane!'

As the door closed behind her they stared at one another in silence. It struck Jamie that for once Jake was not totally relaxed and in control. Even the way he walked seemed less smooth than normal.

Standing a few feet away from her, he proffered the cardboard box. 'A peace offering and your wedding present.' His voice sounded slightly unfamiliar, husky almost.

Numbly Jamie took the box from him. Ridiculously she knew that tears weren't very far away. A wedding present from him had been the last thing she had expected—or wanted, and yet her fingers trembled as she put the box on her bed and opened it.

The fur revealed when she finally got past the layers of tissue paper made her gasp in shocked amazement.

The jacket was styled casually with a hood and a blouson body that would be ideal for skiing in, although the luxurious dark grey fox pelts were far too luxurious to expose to the icy ski-slopes. She picked it up with hands that trembled, suddenly aware that Jake was frowning.

'If you don't like it . . .'

For once the sharp acidity of his voice didn't hurt her. 'I love it, Jake,' she told him quietly. Quickly she put it on, marvelling at its perfect fit. The dark glossy fur was a perfect foil for her colouring. She opened her mouth to thank him, and then the door opened and Beth hurried in.

'My goodness!' she admired, studying Jamie enviously. 'How lovely, but you'll have to thank him for it later, Jamie,' she told her cousin, 'otherwise you're going to miss your plane.'

Jake was driving them to the airport himself, and leaving his car there so that he could pick it up when they returned.

'We'll have to start house-hunting when we get back,' he commented as he drove into the airport complex. 'The flat's okay for now, but it won't do once we have a family.' He parked the car expertly, and helped Jamie out. A porter came to take their luggage, and as Jake caught hold of her arm, the reality of what she had committed herself to hit Jamie properly for the first time.

She had never liked flying and today was no exception, her one desire being to go to sleep and wake up only when they were safely down on the ground again. The take-off reduced her to a ball of tense screaming nerves that relaxed only when Jake prised her clenched fingers off the arm rest and clasped her hand in his own.

He shook his head when the stewardess offered them something to drink, and Jamie refused likewise when the girl came round a little later with their meal. Her stomach was churning far too much to allow her to eat. Jake refused his meal as well, and as she studied him covertly while his attention was on the stewardess, she ached with the anguish of all that their marriage was not and could never be. If only she could turn the clock back six years to before she had learned the truth. If only he loved her as she loved him. But he didn't.

'Something wrong?'

She hadn't realised he was looking at her, and a deep blush burned up over her body, colouring her skin. 'No, nothing.' Her tongue touched her lips in a give-away nervous motion. 'I was miles away...'

'Thinking about your lover?' She watched his face darken, absorbing his words with a faint sense of shock. 'Well, you won't be thinking about him tonight,' he told her softly. 'I promise you that much, Jamie.'

After the flight came the hour-long taxi drive up to their resort. Jamie sat through it in an exhausted silence that Jake made no attempt to interrupt.

Although she could ski Jamie had never visited Jake's favourite resort before. It was too dark to see anything of their surroundings when the driver dropped them off at the entrance to the hotel. As Jake ushered her inside she had a brief impression of a comfortable foyer, very traditional in appearance, with the sort of floors and furnishings that would not be damaged by snow-covered boots and clothes.

At one end of the room a group of people were clustered round a roaring log fire, chatting and drinking, their smart ski-wear suggesting that the hotel was both exclusive and expensive. French seemed to be the dominant language spoken, perhaps not unexpected when the hotel was French-owned.

Jamie stood to one side while Jake talked to the receptionist. A key changed hands, then Jake turned back to her.

'Our chalet's all ready. Someone is taking the luggage over for us. This way.' He took her back outside, the sharp coldness of the air after the warmth of the hotel making her shiver.

A horse-drawn sleigh waited just by the door and Jake handed her into it, deftly tucking a warm plaid rug round her legs as the driver set the sleigh in motion. The horses' bridles carried small bells that rang as they moved, snow hissing beneath the sleigh runners.

'It's the quickest and cheapest form of transport,' Jake told her when she marvelled at the speed at which the horses travelled along the snow-packed track. 'Our chalet is one of the furthest from the hotel—it's completely self-sufficient, but of course all the hotel facilities are available to us should we want them. I thought you'd prefer to have dinner in the chalet this evening.' He glanced at his watch, 'It's almost seven-thirty now. I've ordered it for half eight.'

They had passed several of the square wooden chalets before the horses stopped outside one, standing patiently while the driver unloaded their luggage and carried it towards the chalet.

Traditionally constructed of logs, the upper storey had a small balcony from which Jamie guessed there would be a marvellous view of the valley and the snowfields when it was light.

The sleigh driver opened the door and carried in their cases. Jake ushered Jamie inside, then turned to tip the silent man. The door opened straight on to a comfortably sized square room, with a polished wood floor, scattered with what looked like goatskin rugs. A fire burned cheerfully in the stone fireplace, two comfortable chairs and a settee upholstered in a nubble tweed fabric formed the room's main furniture. A row of shelves on the wall by the fireplace held a television set and a telephone, and open-tread wooden stairs led to the upper storey.

'Kitchen's through there,' Jake told her, gesturing to a door in the far wall. 'You can check it out later. Right now, we've just got time to change for dinner.'

'Change?' Jamie stared at his back as he carried their cases upstairs. Since he had said they would be eating in the chalet she had expected that they would eat informally, but Jake it seemed had other ideas.

Wearily she followed him upstairs. Only one door opened off the small landing, and she pushed it inwards and walked through. Jake was standing in front of the fire warming his hands, and Jamie looked at her surroundings curiously.

The bedroom was pleasantly large, the bed... The bed was very generously proportioned, she thought faintly, and very high with what looked like enormously plump pillows and an equally thick duvet. A row of wardrobes and cupboards ran along one wall and in addition to the bed the room was furnished with a table and two comfortable armchairs and a small writing-desk. On the wall adjacent to the bed was another door which Jamie decided must lead into the bathroom. She walked over to it, and opened the door, her eyes widening in bemusement at what she saw. She was unaware that Jake had come to stand behind her, until she felt the vibrations of his voice against her ear.

'It's a jacuzzi,' he told her softly, following the direction of her gaze. 'And very therapeutic and relaxing it is, too, after a hard day's skiing.'

'I'm sure,' Jamie agreed hardily, withdrawing from the room and closing the door, knowing even as she did so that the images that had tormented her mind as she looked into the bathroom were not going to be ones she would find it easy to live with. From Jake's easy familiarity with the chalet either it was one he had occupied before, or he had stayed in one that was similar. And no doubt he hadn't stayed here alone, she thought jealously, her mind re-conjuring erotic images of Jake's naked brown body, tangling intimately in the bubbling waters of that generously proportioned jacuzzi with that of some unknown female companion. Oh yes, she had no doubt at all that Jake would find it extremely relaxing and therapeutic to make love in the languorous heat of those bubbling waters. Jealousy boiled up inside her, her body tense with the effort of suppressing it.

'Do you want to shower first or shall I?' Jake asked casually, interrupting her tormenting thoughts.

'You go ahead. I'll have a look round. You're obviously a lot more familiar with the chalet than I am.'

'The layout's the same as one I've stayed in before with some friends, although this one's smaller,' he offered. 'I've never stayed in this one before. The privacy it affords has never been something I've particularly wanted on previous skiing trips,' he added mockingly.

So at least he hadn't brought another woman here, Jamie thought achingly, as he disappeared into the bathroom, and she started on the task of unpacking her case.

The last thing she felt like doing was going through the farce of changing for a dinner she didn't really want, but it was easier to go along with what Jake wanted than to go through the exhausting process of arguing with him.

He wasn't long in the shower, emerging with wet hair and clad in a thick towelling bathrobe. Fear and excitement clutched at her stomach. She felt as nervous as a virgin with her first man, she thought irately. But then sne had been, and he was her first and quite possibly her last, certainly her only lover. But he didn't know that, and he wasn't going to know it, she reminded herself as she gathered up clean underwear and headed for the bathroom without looking at him.

She was as brief as he had been, emerging into the bedroom to find him dressed in dark trousers and a white dinner-shirt. He paused to look at her as he inserted cufflinks into the cuffs, and as she looked at them Jamie realised they were the ones she had bought for him. As he looked at her, her throat closed up, tension invading her body. He took a step towards her, and then a bell shrilled somewhere downstairs, making her jump.

'No doubt that will be our dinner,' Jake said calmly. 'I'll go down and let them in.'

In view of Jake's formal choice of clothing Jamie felt obliged to follow suit. No doubt if she really had been a bride, she would have chosen to don an exotic and very feminine négligé of some sort, but even had she wanted to there was no such item in her wardrobe. A couple of brief satin nightshirts with low scooped necks, short sleeves and shirt tails comprised her only sleep wear, and if Jake didn't like them he could...he could... Her body trembled as she tried not to think of what he could and all too likely would do, to register his disapproval, her hands moving agitatedly through the contents of her case until she found the simple jersey dress she had decided to wear.

The warm cream fabric suited her skin, the narrow tubular dress hugging her slender body to fall in soft folds at her feet. Long tight sleeves covered her arms, the slightly scooped neckline revealing the delicacy of her bones. Deftly applying the minimum of make-up, Jamie found her shoes and went downstairs.

A damask-covered round table had been pulled up in front of the fire, two chairs which she presumed had come from the kitchen placed opposite one another. An ice-bucket containing a bottle of wine and some champagne stood beside the table. Jake, she saw, was bending to plug in a covered trolley which she presumed contained their dinner. He stood up and saw her, his eyes narrowing over her as he studied her.

'Why is it that something that covers you so modestly from head to foot should so explicitly remind me of exactly how you look without a stitch of clothing?'

The cool conversational tone in which he spoke rendered her completely unable to reply. With one simple sentence he had destroyed every barrier she had tried to erect between them in choosing to wear such a demure dress, and she could only stare at him with hunted eyes as he came towards her, proffering a glass of champagne.

CHAPTER EIGHT

'MORE champagne?'

She had already had two full glasses, so stifling the cowardly impulse to say 'Yes', Jamie shook her head, and stopped toying with her chocolate mousse.

She had barely touched her meal—barely eaten anything all day, in fact, and despite being cautious in what she had had to drink she already felt distinctly light-headed. It would be the easiest thing in the world to let Jake give her enough champagne to render her oblivious to everything but the pleasure of his possession, but she didn't want it that way. Pride, the same pride that had made her run from him in the first place, refused to let her hide behind the numbing effect of too much champagne.

She stood up a little unsteadily, tensing as Jake helped her with her chair. Mark was the old-fashioned kind of man who believed in all the small courtesies to the female sex, and while she doubted that Jake was anywhere near as chivalrous as his father his manners were always impeccable.

'I'm rather tired, I think I'll go to bed now.'

Lord, how difficult it was to say the words, her eyes fastening on anything rather than look into Jake's face.

As Jake stepped smoothly to one side to allow her to pass, the firelight glinted on the diamonds in his cufflinks, and Jamie shuddered inwardly. He had worn them on purpose, she knew that. But for what purpose?

She didn't look back as she climbed the stairs, but she was aware of Jake standing in the room below with every tensed muscle. No doubt he was enjoying this, she thought bitterly, but it was all he would enjoy. If he touched her... If. Didn't she mean when? And what would she do? Fight him off? He had at least twice her physical strength. Lie cold and unmoving beneath him? Would that she could.

She hadn't lied when she claimed that she was tired. The hectic build-up to the wedding; the emotional traumas she had gone through in the last few weeks; the fact that she had barely eaten for the last three days had all combined to drain her fragile reserves of energy.

Now it was an effort even to move; her body ached from the flight and the bumpy taxi-journey to the resort. All she wanted to do was to soak her tiredness away in a long hot bath and then crawl into bed.

She found her nightshirt and her toilet things and walked into the bathroom, pleased to see that it was equipped with a conventional bath as well as the partitioned-off jacuzzi.

The bathroom door didn't possess a lock—it obviously wasn't considered necessary in a one-bedroomed chalet.

What was the matter with her? she asked herself as she ran water into the bath and stripped off her clothes. Jake was hardly likely to come barging in. No, he was far too subtle for that. And besides, she suspected he was enjoying drawing out her torment.

It was all so silly. When she had first learned that he intended to marry her, it had been the emotional side of their relationship she had feared; after all, they had already been lovers; she already knew his body as intimately as she knew her own. It was ridiculous to feel so nervous and *distrait*, much more so now than at eighteen when she had after all been a totally inexperienced virgin. But then of course she had thought she had Jake's love; she had felt secure and protected; whereas now... Now she felt vulnerable and threatened.

There was a glass jar of rose-scented bath-crystals beside the bath and she tipped some into the bath. The delicate scent was released by the heat of the water, water which felt silky soft against her skin. Sighing, she relaxed into the water. It was bliss. She could have stayed there for ever. She closed her eyes tiredly, and then opened them wide as she heard the bedroom door open.

In a flash she was out of the bath, drying herself quickly with a thick fluffy towel. Her heart pounded feverishly, but the bathroom door remained closed.

Tugging her nightshirt over her still slightly damp skin, Jamie picked up her discarded clothes and stared at the bathroom door. Shrugging fatalistically, she walked towards it. She couldn't stay here all night, after all.

Jake was sitting in front of the fire, apparently reading a newspaper. He looked up as he heard the bathroom door and studied her. No doubt he found her deep blue satin nightshirt less than bridal, she thought wryly, but if he thought she was going to get herself dolled up in layers of chiffon and lace... He had removed the jacket he had worn during dinner and unfastened the top studs of his shirt. Looking at him, Jamie was suddenly conscious of how much taller he was than her when she wasn't wearing high heels. He was looking at her rather oddly, frowning almost.

'You look about seventeen in that get-up.'

The taunting mockery of his voice angered her. To get to the bed she had to walk past him, and she did so determinedly, her voice cold as she responded, 'But I'm not, am I?'

He smiled as he let her walk past him, but the sensation of his eyes on her back made her skin prickle with atavistic warnings. His hand came out, imprisoning her wrist, swinging her round to face him. The movement brought a flash of fire from his cufflinks, and watching her following it he smiled again.

'I still haven't thanked you properly for them, have I?'

Tiny tremors of alarm ran down her spine. Neither his eyes nor his voice betrayed anything but she knew what he meant.

'I told you—they were *my* payment to *you*.'

She forced herself to meet his eyes, but almost flinched from the glittering fury she saw in them.

'You're *too* generous. In fact so generous that you leave me feeling in your debt. And debts must always be repaid, mustn't they, Jamie?'

She wanted to swallow the ball of fright that had lodged in her throat, but her rigid muscles wouldn't let her. Still gripping her wrist with one hand, Jake used the other to free the links from his shirt. Without taking his eyes from her face he placed them on the coffee-table beside his chair.

'Look at me.'

Unwillingly she shifted her glance from the cufflinks to his face.

'That's better.' The smile that curled his mouth made her want to shudder, but she kept her body tensed, braced against the fear rioting through her. She should never have given in to the impulse to buy him those cufflinks. She should have realised he would never let her get away with the implied insult.

Without being able to do a thing about it she felt him draw her towards him. Both his hands held her now, curling round her upper arms just where the short sleeves of her nightshirt ended. As she felt the heat of his body encompass her she pulled back, arching her spine away from the contact.

She wanted to break down and plead with him not to do this to her, not to destroy her memories, and she knew that she only had to open her mouth and he would stop. But once again that fierce, terrible pride that had been her downfall so often in the past wouldn't let her utter the words. Jake wanted to humble and humiliate her. He wanted her to weep and beg. Every nerve-ending she possessed screamed at her to escape, but even if he had let her go she doubted if she could have moved. Over and above logic and reality ran a dark tide of compulsion to know just once more what it would be like to be held in his arms.

The knowledge shocked through her, darkening her eyes, making Jake's fingers dig into her flesh as though he knew what she was thinking.

He bent his head towards her. She knew that he was going to kiss her and all at once her courage deserted her. She arched her throat back, turning her head away, shuddering when she felt one arm go round her waist, pulling her against his body, while the other cupped the back of her neck, hard fingers pressing against her spine. She held her breath as she felt his mouth feather lightly against her throat, her senses recoiling from the effect of his touch. She reeled under the impact of the sensations he was arousing inside her, shocked by the reality of her vulnerability to him. Her body shivered and his mouth stilled on the frantic pulse it had found.

'Let me go, Jake!'

She got the words out from an aching throat, clenching her muscles against any response to him.

'You say the words, but they have no meaning,' she heard him mock, his mouth close to her ear. 'Your body wants me as its lover, Jamie.'

'No!'

The anguished, hoarse denial tore at her sore throat, but the only effect her anguish had on Jake was to make him even more angry.

'Yes,' he hissed into her skin, removing his hand from her nape to run it insolently down her body from her shoulder, over the breast, into the curve of her waist and against the fullness of her hip and then back again to linger mockingly where her nipple pressed wantonly against the satin fabric. The traitorous response of her body to his lightest touch was its own betrayal.

'Stop it, Jake!'

'Never.' The harshness of his denial shocked her. She stared up at him, her senses registering the thick sound suppressed in his throat as his hand covered her breast and his mouth found hers with a savage force that blasted away her resistance.

This was what she wanted, she knew hazily, this was what she had ached and pined for, this primitive hunger; this matchless sense of wanting and being wanted. The pressure of Jake's mouth deepened to a hot, drugging passion that obliterated everything else. Somehow her arms were round his neck, her body arching up to his as the pressure of his mouth bent her head backwards, and his lips demanded that she give up to him every last bit of her mouth's sweetness.

Jamie felt her body melting achingly into Jake's as his mouth caressed her skin, finding all the secret pleasure spots only he knew.

The years rolled back, reality was forgotten, her neck arching eagerly beneath the teasing exploration of his lips. His hands were on her back, her breasts flattened against his chest. As his hands slid down to her hips she felt the hardness of his arousal against her and shuddered achingly.

He was playing with her now, she recognised dimly as he teased a line of kisses against the scooped neckline of her nightshirt, arousing her in ways that her body remembered even if her mind wanted to forget.

She withstood the torment for as long as she could, his name a long moan of need that burst from her throat as her body shuddered in violent responsiveness to the skilled seduction of his mouth and hands. She felt his hands on her nightshirt, lifting it from her body, and suddenly ached with the need to be free of it. Firelight warmed her skin to soft amber, the glitter in Jake's eyes as he studied the curves of her body taking her back in time. She had known that look before, known the fierce passion that went with it, and her body ached to know it again.

'Jamie!'

She shuddered at the harsh, raw need in his voice, suppressing a soft moan of pleasure as his fingers drifted softly over the fire-illuminated outline of her breasts. Tormented by the need exploding inside her, she arched back beneath his caress, offering the aching fullness of her breasts to him in a wanton mixture of challenge and appeal. His breath rattled thickly in his throat, his skin hot against her own as he picked her up and carried her to the chair, sitting down with her in his arms.

They had been like this once before, although then she had not been undressed as she now was. They had been alone in the library at home. Jake had unfastened the buttons of her shirt—with fingers that trembled in much the same way as they trembled now. And then he had put his mouth to her breast and . . .

She breathed in on a sharp sob of pleasure as she felt the tentative caress of his tongue against her tender flesh, but with her memories of the past to torment her it was not enough. Her fingers curled into his shoulder beneath his open shirt, her teeth nipping sharply at his skin as her body arched in aching supplication against his mouth.

His hand cupped her breast, his mouth closing fiercely on its aching peak, sucking, tugging, biting in a frantic rhythm that soothed her husky moans of need.

In the past there had been passion between them, but it had never reached this tormented, feverish pitch. His need of her might not have anything to do with love, but it was there, she recognised, running her fingers down his chest, tugging open the rest of his shirt buttons, wanting to arouse him to the same impossible pitch to which he had aroused her.

His mouth found her other breast, and Jamie tugged impatiently at the fastening of his trousers, sliding her hand across the hot tensed flesh of his stomach.

'Jamie...' His voice shook with repressed frustration, his chest rising and falling sharply as he fought for self-control, trapping her hand before she could touch him more intimately. 'It was bad enough before, but now...' She saw him shake his head, the firelight highlighting the hot colour of his skin. 'You've got me as aroused and impatient as a teenage boy!'

The words were groaned from a throat suddenly rigid with tension, as she moved her hand, dragging her nails lightly through the dark silky line of body hair, his chest expanding as he fought to draw in air. He didn't try to stop her when she stroked her fingers along the hard outline of his arousal, her whole body shaking with the need he had aroused, moving instead more easily to accommodate her touch.

'Jamie.' His voice was muffled as he buried his head against her breasts, but the aching tension in it was unmistakable. It gave her a heady sense of power and freedom. She teased him gently, tasting the salt-flavoured beads of perspiration that sprang up on his skin, letting her tongue stroke tantalisingly along his shoulder.

Suddenly she was lying on the rug before the fire, with Jake arching over her as he tugged off the rest of his clothes. His body was just as she remembered it, superbly male; but the expression in his eyes was different. Before he had always retained some element of control, but now surprisingly she saw that he had none. His eyes glittered darkly as he leaned over her, her body trembling softly in anticipation of its long-desired possession by his. What was happening to her was something outside reason and logic, something elemental and, she could almost believe, pre-ordained. She no longer wanted to resist him; had stopped wanting to in fact almost from the first moment he touched her, and now she felt no shame or humiliation in lifting her mouth to his skin and letting her lips play softly over his chest while her hands caressed the well remembered shape of his body.

A fine sheen of sweat gilded his skin, so dark and tanned against the paleness of her own. His hands trapped hers, holding them against his hips.

'No more, Jamie,' he demanded thickly, his voice husky with male arousal, and then his mouth was on hers, his body pressing hers into the soft rug.

'How many other men have seen you like this?' he demanded shockingly when at last he released her swollen mouth. 'Touched you like this, or this?' He was reducing her to a mass of quivering fire, her blood running at fever heat, melting her bones, the ache spreading through her obliterating everything else, so that she was clinging to him, arching her hips against the tormenting stroke of his hand, mutely begging for release.

Kneeling above her, Jake looked almost barbaric in the firelight. 'How many, Jamie? How many made you feel as I do?'

His hand touched her intimately, eliciting a response that sent tiny shock waves shimmering through her. She closed her eyes childishly, wanting to blot out his words and concentrate only on sensations, but his touch, initially so satisfying, had become a torment.

When she opened her eyes he was looking back at her, demanding her admission that he alone could do this to her, wanting it, she realised, needing it almost. It amazed her that someone as arrogant and strong as Jake should betray such vulnerability, and without thinking she reached up to touch his face, her voice soft as she told him honestly, 'No one makes me feel the way you can, Jake. No one.'

She saw him shudder with tension, his own voice thick and hoarse as he moved between her legs, his hands sliding to her hips, lifting and supporting her, his mouth against her ear as he muttered rawly, 'And no one can make me feel the way you do either, Jamie.'

It was the last admission she had expected, but the shock of hearing it was lost beneath the devastating pleasure of the slow thrust of his body into her own. His fingers tangled in her hair, holding her head pinioned as his mouth closed with hot urgency on her own, her hips lifted to hold him, her legs wrapping his body.

'I want you . . . I want you . . . I want you.'

The harsh words fell sweetly on her ears as Jake abandoned his self-control, his body possessed by the driving force of his desire.

Shockingly there was a brief moment of pain as her own flesh, unaccustomed to the act of possession, yielded to his maleness. But her need for him was too intense to be suppressed for long, her body gloriously matching and sharing the tumultuous rhythm of his to explode finally in a series of sweetly agonising contractions that took him with her beyond the limits of human experience to a place where no one existed except themselves.

On the verge of total exhaustion, Jamie was tiredly aware of Jake carrying her to their bed, of the softness of the duvet being tucked almost tenderly around her, although that must surely have been an illusion. If so it was one she was too content and at peace to question. She had given herself to Jake with love and had shared with him the ultimate human experience. He wanted her enough to need to know that what she shared with him she had shared with no other man, and that must mean something.

Some time during the night she had a dream that she was losing him, the devastation of that loss making her cry out his name sharply, waking herself up. She was alone in the huge bed. She shivered convulsively.

'Jamie, are you all right?'

Jake was standing by the fire, feeding it with logs.

'I...' Why on earth couldn't she drag her eyes from his naked body? She licked her lips nervously, remembering her earlier betraying response to him. 'I had a bad dream.' She wasn't going to tell him what it was. She watched him walk back to the bed and get in beside her. When he took her in his arms her heart leapt in shock.

'Try and get back to sleep.' His touch was that of a re-assuring adult to a child, his breath warm against her skin as he tucked her head into his shoulder. She wanted to pull away and yet shamingly she wanted to stay, to ab-sorb this precious sense of being close to him. Tiredness washed over her and she closed her eyes, letting herself drift back into sleep.

But the dream wouldn't go away, and this time when she cried out the sound was smothered against Jake's skin, her cry of anguished despair sobbed into his throat, the sensation of his flesh against her mouth bringing her sharply awake.

At first she thought he was still asleep, but then he said quietly,

'Jamie, what is it?'

How could she tell him that she cried in her sleep be-cause she was frightened of losing him? Despair washed over her. After only a few short hours in his arms she was back where she had been at eighteen, vulnerable and trapped in a love that he didn't want.

Ridiculously she felt tears welling in her eyes, over-flowing and dampening Jake's skin. He moved abruptly, his hand cupping her face and holding it still as he looked into her eyes.

'Have I done this to you?'

He sounded so unexpectedly humble that she could only stare at him.

'It needn't be a bad marriage, Jamie,' he told her softly. 'I think tonight's already proved that. Physically we still want one another.' He frowned as though suddenly remembering something. 'You tensed and cried out when I made love to you. That was a very odd reaction from a woman who's as experienced as you. It was almost like the first time I possessed you,' he added musingly, 'when you were still a virgin.' He paused and then looked at her for a long time, and then probed softly, 'How many other men have there been since me, Jamie?'

Frantically she turned her head away, her heart pounding. Had he guessed that *he* was the only one? Desperately she looked for a means of self-defence.

'How many, Jamie?'

'I can't remember.'

'You're lying. There haven't been *any*, have there?'

His perception stunned her into silence for a second, the look in his eyes making her shake with self-loathing. He felt sorry for her, pitied her.

'All right, so there haven't been any,' she told him furiously, 'but don't let that swell your ego, Jake, it wasn't because I couldn't bear to replace you. It was because I couldn't bear the thought of being cheated by another man, the way you cheated me. You spoiled me for other men, Jake.'

There was another long silence while the tension stretched between them, then he said slowly,

'Then you'll just have to be satisfied with what I can give you, won't you?'

And this time when he took her in his arms she did struggle, but it wasn't any use. His mouth and hands

subdued her, not by force but by skilfully using against
her her own desires.

The sensual brush of his mouth and hands against her
skin induced a voluptuous sense of languor. His tongue
skimmed her nipples and ripples of pleasure spread
through her body. Her flesh seemed acutely sensitised by
his touch, the lazy ripples intensifying in depth and urgency as his lips moved delicately over her stomach,
finding the hollows against her hip-bones. Suddenly she
was very hot, her skin burning, damp with the prickles of
perspiration breaking out on it, the languor gone, the
swift resurgence of desire making her move restlessly
against Jake's touch.

He made a sound in his throat, a primitive male growl
of appreciation. His fingers touched the fine, silky tri-
angle of hair between her thighs and she shuddered, her
stomach muscles locking in a fierce spasm of desire.

She wanted to touch him, but he was out of reach, the
satin sheen of his skin highlighted by the fire as he
moved, pushing back the duvet until it fell off the bed.
Her body ached with primitive need, tense with the frustration of the unwanted cessation of her pleasure. She
wanted to tell him how she felt, but the words were impossible to form. Part of her still felt the same inhibi-
tions she had felt before he had made love to her. It was
a strange sensation, something she had not experienced
with him before, but then she had been young and un-
knowing, willing to follow where he led; her body dom-
inated by the magic his wrought upon it. Now her flesh
was making its own demands.

She wanted him to come back to her, to take her in his arms and fill her body with the hard heat of his flesh, but instead he knelt at the bottom of the bed, his palm cupping her foot, his thumb stroking slowly over her toes. She quivered involuntarily in response to his touch, her toes curling protestingly. His bulk blocked out the light from the fire, his expression hidden from her.

He had been pleased by her admission that she had had no other lovers. It angered her that she had made it, but she had wiped the pleasure from his eyes with her taunt that he had turned her off men for life. All men but one, she recognised numbly, shivering beneath the slow caress of his mouth against her skin.

His tongue investigated the sensitive nerve endings behind her knee, her muscles locking treacherously as she drew in a sharp breath. His fingers caressed the inside of her thigh, turning her muscles to liquid jelly. Hot quivers of pleasure burned her skin, her mind trying to deny the effect he was having on her at the same time as her body ached for more.

A pulse beat feverishly deep inside her. A small moan that could have been delight or despair was torn from her throat. She wanted him to stop. She wanted him to go on. He had touched her like this before, but never without letting her touch him, without absorbing with his own body some of her frantic need for release.

Quickening ripples of desire gripped her muscles and his hand moved to lie against her stomach to register its subtle quiver. The loss of his intimate touch made her tense with frustration. Perspiration soaked her skin, her nails curling painfully into her palms as she moved her head frantically from side to side on the pillow, and she closed her eyes as she moaned his name. What was he trying to do to her?

'Tell me you want me.'

His voice was harsh with tension, contradicting her belief that he was totally unmoved by her arousal. The hand that was spread against her stomach tautened. For a moment she was tempted to deny him—and herself— but for once her desire was stronger than her pride. Whether she said the words or not, her body had already betrayed her.

'I want you.'

The words seemed to be dragged from some place deep inside her, hurting her throat and making her eyes prickle with unwanted tears. Just saying them seemed to relax her almost unbearable tension; a dull sense of misery overwhelming her desire. She suddenly shivered, disliking both herself and Jake. It was her sniping and bitterness that had brought him to punishing her like this. She moved beneath his hand, intending to drag herself away, her misery pierced shockingly by the pressure of Jake's hands pushing her back against the bed, his voice raw with an emotion that was unfamiliar to her as he muttered against her skin,

'Not half as much as I want you.'

And then his tongue moved delicately against her sensitive flesh, caressing her with exquisite care. All the breath seemed to quit her lungs at once, leaving her gasping for air, her intended protest lost beneath the sharp high sob of pleasure that rasped her throat.

She wanted him to stop; she wanted to escape the flush of moist heat engulfing her body; to evade the pulsing rhythm passing from his mouth to her flesh, but more than any of this she wanted him to go on inducing the frantic pleasure absorbing her.

Her hips writhed and twisted in his hands, possessed of a life divorced from her mind, the hoarse sharp sounds of pleasure splintering from her throat as unfamiliar to her as the intimacy of his caress. Her body lifted, arching eagerly towards the source of its pleasure, and he seemed to like her responsiveness to him, his mouth suddenly hot and demanding against her flesh, enforcing on it a fierce rhythm that beat frantically through her blood, making the world explode into tingling shock waves of sensation that mingled with her sharp cries of pleasure until it became too much to bear and darkness overwhelmed her.

Her body felt weak, completely boneless, her skin damp, her mind still grappling with the shock of her arousal. Jake moved and she felt the rough brush of his tongue against her belly. It was like being licked by a giant cat, Jamie thought drowsily, feeling her skin grow warm and relax as life flowed back into her drained body. He made a sound in his throat that was almost a purr; a sexy male sound of satisfaction and pleasure. He had enjoyed what he had just done to her, she realised in astonished wonderment. He had liked the sensation of her body completely abandoning itself to him. His tongue still stroked her skin, his hands sliding firmly over her body.

He reached her breasts and caressed them slowly, lingering over his self-imposed task until unbelievably she could feel an unmistakable surge of desire sweep through her. Her nipple hardened under his tongue, her fingers locking behind his nape as her body tensed.

As though it was what he had been waiting for, he buried his mouth in her throat, kissing it fiercely. Her body, acutely responsive to everything about him, arched in frantic invitation, her mouth finding the hard warmth of his shoulder and sucking feverishly on it as though she couldn't get enough of the taste and feel of him.

He made a harsh sound of pleasure against her throat, lifting his head to look into her eyes. The world stood still as he slowly moved his body against hers, his eyes refusing to let her look away.

It shocked her that she could be so moist and eager for his possession, her flesh clinging hotly to his as though obsessed by the need to be filled with it.

'This is how it is between us,' he muttered hoarsely, letting his body fill her. 'And this time I'm not letting you throw it all away.'

His throat moved, and she felt the tension in him, the supreme self-control. She touched her tongue to his throat, absorbing the tiny bead of sweat that clung to his Adam's apple, and almost instantly his control shattered, his mouth possessing hers with something close to savagery. He probed her lips, his body moving rhythmically within hers, driving them both towards the outer reaches of human control. Fierce quivers of spasmodic pleasure erupted inside her, making Jake groan her name against the soft skin of her throat and then move demandingly within her, his body shuddering into release as it was gripped by the spiralling convulsions of her muscles.

It took her several seconds to realise that the harsh alien sound tormenting her ears was Jake's tortured breathing. His weight lay slumped against her, threatening to crack her ribs, but ridiculously she didn't want him to move away. She wanted to wrap her arms around him and keep him close to her for ever, and not just because of the pleasure his body could give hers, pleasure that had almost frightened her by its intensity, she acknowledged mutely.

He moved, and she subdued the small protest tormenting her throat. She felt him push her hair back off her hot face before he pulled the duvet back over them both. His arms held her against his body, her face resting against his throat. She nuzzled it softly with her lips, liking the salt-sweat taste of his skin.

'Do you know how long it's been since anyone made me feel like that?' His half-slurred words made Jamie tense. She didn't want to be compared with his other women, to be awarded an 'A' for effort. She pulled out of his arms and turned over, keeping her back towards him.

'Jamie?'

His hand touched her nape and she froze and moved away.

'I'm tired and I want to sleep. You've proved your point, Jake,' she told him bitterly, 'but I don't have to listen to you gloat about it.'

She felt him turn away and knew she had got what she wanted, but stupidly she ached to be back in his arms, to have the illusion of believing that he cared. Not even the thickness of the duvet could melt the icy chill that seemed to have invaded her heart.

CHAPTER NINE

WHEN Jamie woke up in the morning she was alone. She opened her eyes and then rolled over, vivid mental images more eloquent than a thousand words flashing accusingly behind her eyes. She had let Jake make love to her. No, she had *wanted* Jake to make love to her. Wanted him and shown him that wanting. She groaned and burrowed deeper into the pillows, tensing as her senses registered the faint male scent that clung to the linen. She was lying on Jake's pillow manoeuvring her body into the space that he had left. God, was there no end to her folly? And where was he, this new husband of hers who had shown her so graphically and unrelentingly last night the exact nature of the relationship between them?

How easily he managed to deceive everyone else. Beth, Mark, her mother, all of them thought he was wonderful. Her mother was always describing him as honourable and highly principled. For God's sake, what was principled about a man who deliberately chose to reduce a woman to sensual slavery simply as a means of punishment?

She turned over and lay on her back, her hands behind her head. The chalet had an empty feeling that suggested Jake had gone out. She tried not to feel mournful and deserted.

Last night ... She closed her eyes and tried to breathe slowly. Last night there had been desire in his touch as well as skill. She moved restlessly beneath the duvet. Why was she trying to find excuses for him? Okay, so he had wanted her, but that was no excuse for the kind of intimacy he had forced upon her. Forced, mocked a wry inner voice, but she ignored it, concentrating on her main pattern of thought. That kind of intimacy was for lovers, something precious that only two people who truly loved should share.

Mocking herself for her prudishness, she got out of bed, shivering as the cold air struck her. The bedroom fire had gone out. She showered quickly and then dressed in cord jeans and a thick sweater.

Downstairs the fire was in, the evidence of last night's meal gone. Jamie walked into the kitchen. Jake had written her a note and propped it up against the coffee-pot.

'Maid has been—told her not to disturb you,' he had written. 'Breakfast things are in fridge. Meet you at lunchtime in the hotel bar.'

A pretty casual note to leave for a brand-new wife, Jamie thought morosely, making herself a pot of coffee. She glanced at her watch. It was gone eleven.

Now in the daylight she could see the ski slopes and the small village down in the valley. She wandered into the sitting-room and opened the front door, glad to see that she could see the hotel from it. It was probably less than half a mile away—not a long walk.

Having drunk her coffee, she pulled on her boots and set off in the direction of the hotel.

The road, which had been in darkness the previous evening, wound pleasantly through several small stands of firs, the other chalets set back from it in small groups. On the opposite side of the valley were what Jamie suspected were the nursery slopes, very busy at this time of the morning with brightly clad ski-suited figures. Jake would probably have taken the ski lift to one of the more difficult runs.

A pretty brunette with a warm smile directed Jamie towards the bar when she stopped at the hotel reception and also gave her a local map which included all the ski-runs graded accordingly.

It was almost twelve-thirty and the bar was full. Jamie ordered herself a drink and was lucky enough to find a table that had just been vacated. Most of the other people seemed to be in groups of fours or sixes, the snatches of conversation she overheard confirming what Jake had already told her about the resort; namely that it was run for skiers, rather than those more devoted to *après-ski*, and that the same people tended to come back year after year.

From her vantage point with a good view of the door, she saw Jake before he saw her. His black ski-suit emphasised the lean hardness of his body and she felt her pulses race responsively. He turned his head, his face already tanned by the alpine sun. Jamie was just about to call out to him when she saw the woman with him.

Instantly her body froze, panic filling her in case he turned and saw her. What was he doing with Wanda? What was Wanda doing here anyway? They were talking with the familiarity of old acquaintances—old lovers, she thought bitterly, and then Jake turned his head and saw her, and it was too late for her to escape unseen.

He came towards her, Wanda hanging back slightly. When he reached the table he bent his head, capturing her mouth in a brief hard kiss, his fingers warm against her nape.

As he raised his head she saw that he was grinning. 'Come and say hello to my lazy bride, Wanda.'

His total lack of embarrassment or guilt was oddly more hurtful than the fact that he should be with another woman—no, not just *another* woman, Jamie reminded herself, but the woman who had once told her that Jake didn't love her and why. Did they always come here to Switzerland at the same time, or had they met today simply by coincidence?

The other woman stepped forward. She looked older, Jamie acknowledged, her smile slightly wary. She seemed to have lost the brittle self-confidence Jamie remembered so well.

'Jamie.'

'I bumped into Wanda by the ski-lifts this morning and invited her to have lunch with us,' Jake explained, pulling out a chair for the other woman and then asking them both what they wanted to drink.

Jamie shook her head; her glass was still half full.

'Nothing for me either.' Wanda patted her stomach with a rueful smile. 'Junior here doesn't seem to approve of alcohol.' She moved her hand and Jamie saw the glint of gold on her wedding-ring finger.

Maybe their meeting had been innocent after all, or maybe Wanda was simply skilfully trying to deflect her suspicions. Six years ago Wanda had had no compunction at all about telling Jamie that Jake didn't love her and that in fact he was her lover.

'Well, if neither of you want a drink, we might as well go in for lunch,' Jake announced.

He stood back to let them both precede him and Jamie took the opportunity of murmuring coolly to Wanda, 'Is your husband with you?'

'Oh, Gavin's had to go to Innsbruck this morning,' she responded cheerfully. 'An urgent telex arrived from his boss last night, and he's gone to collect some papers. He's a solicitor in the legal department of one of the large multi-nationals and crises are forever boiling up. This is our first proper holiday in three years of marriage, and he only agreed to come away this time because I put pressure on him. He isn't a particularly keen skier.' She wrinkled her nose and turned to smile at Jake.

'Not like Jake. Remember that fantastic run at Corbière when we stayed there five years ago?'

It was said so casually that if Jamie hadn't known the truth she could almost have accepted that they were no more than good friends. Instead red-hot acid jealousy burned into her, her mouth stretching into what she was sure was nothing like a smile as Jake and Wanda continued to reminisce about various ski-runs.

During lunch Wanda virtually monopolised the conversation, although not in any way that Jamie felt able to object to. It was more that her own jealousy and resentment kept her silent, the bitterness inside her far too corrosive to allow her to participate in the good-natured chit-chat Jake and Wanda were exchanging.

Did Wanda's husband know that she and Jake had once been lovers? Had once, or were still? Jamie wondered bitterly. She looked at the other woman, noticing her glowing complexion and contented smile. Did Jake regret that he had not married her when he had the chance? She was already carrying a child—that child could have been the grandson that Mark wanted so desperately.

They were virtually the last ones left in the dining-room when Wanda glanced at her watch and protested wryly,

'Good Lord, that can't possibly be the time! I'll have to go, Jake, I promised I'd meet Gavin in the village at three. Look, why don't the four of us have dinner together tonight?' she suggested as Jake stood up to help her with her chair.

'That's fine by me.' Jake looked at Jamie queryingly and she forced herself to produce a smile.

'We'll meet you in the bar then, eightish,' Wanda suggested. 'See you then.'

Jake was still drinking his coffee, and he drained the cup before saying coolly, 'What's wrong?'

'Nothing.' Why on earth did she have to sound like a truculent child? Jamie thought bitterly.

'If you didn't want to dine with Wanda and her husband you should have said so.'

'I should have thought that since we're on our honeymoon, she wouldn't have asked,' Jamie returned with sarcastic brittleness. 'Or did she take pity on you, thinking you might be bored?'

She saw him raise his eyebrows and regretted the acid comment. If she wasn't careful he would guess that she was jealous—and possibly why.

'Had *I* realised that you were so keen for us to be alone, I wouldn't have accepted,' Jake told her, his mouth twisting in a sardonic smile as he saw her expression.

'Quite. I simply thought you might enjoy the company.'

'Of your ex-girlfriend?'

Watch it, Jamie, she warned herself as she saw his eyebrows lift again. 'Wanda and I never did have much in common,' she told him hastily. 'It could be rather boring for her husband and me to sit and listen to the pair of you reminiscing about the past. I hope he isn't the jealous type.'

'There's nothing for him to be jealous of,' Jake told her imperturbably. 'In spite of what you're hinting, Wanda and I were never anything more than friends.'

She had to grit her teeth to stop herself from calling him a liar. 'Do you want to leave a message at the desk cancelling this evening?' he asked.

She did, but she wasn't going to tell him so. Instead she shrugged her shoulders and said curtly, 'No, don't bother, I suppose it will be better than staying in the chalet by ourselves.'

A shutter seemed to drop over his face as she spoke, his expression suddenly hard and mask-like. In another man the brief tension in his eyes might have suggested that he had been badly hurt, but Jamie knew Jake far better.

'As you say,' he agreed in a metallic voice. 'And I'd hate you to be bored. Of course we could always...'

Any minute now he was going to remind her that she had been far from bored in his arms last night, Jamie thought in a panic-stricken fever, her skin going hot and cold, fear propelling her into unsteady speech.

'We can't spend all our time in bed.'

'I quite agree,' he responded cuttingly. 'That *would* be boring. I was simply going to suggest that we could always split up during the day, if you find my company too enervating.'

'I think that would be a good idea.' Had she gone mad? That was the last thing she wanted, but it was obviously what Jake wanted. 'After all, I've never been a particularly keen skier, and I'd probably only hold you back. You'll get much more pleasure out of skiing with Wanda.'

Why on earth had she added that last bitchy remark? She stood up quickly, almost turning her chair over. Jake got up to help her, his hand steadying her arm, his voice dulcet in her ear as he murmured mockingly,

'You're too modest, Jamie—and you under-estimate yourself.'

She didn't wait to hear any more, pulling away from him and leaving him to settle their bill as she headed for the foyer.

He caught up with her just as she was leaving, frowning slightly as he demanded, 'And just where do you think you're going?'

'Into the village to get myself something to read,' she snapped back. 'Something I don't need your company for, Jake, so please feel free to find something else to do.'

Once more she pulled angrily away from him, seeing his frown turn to anger, the charge of adrenalin her anger had brought her dissipating into sick misery as she watched him turn on his heel and disappear in the direction of the ski-lifts.

In the end she didn't go down to the village. She felt too miserable. Instead she went back to the chalet and curled up in front of the fire in one of the large chairs.

When the doorbell rang she hurried hopefully to answer it, but it wasn't Jake who stood outside, it was Wanda, looking hesitant and very unsure of herself.

'Jake told me you'd gone down to the village, but I noticed the light was on and I thought I'd take a chance and see if you'd come back. Can I talk to you, Jamie?'

'What about?' Jamie asked her stiffly. 'Your relationship with my husband? What's the matter, are you scared I might let the cat out of the bag in front of Gavin?'

She was amazed to see that Wanda coloured hotly, her eyes sliding away from her face.

'Look, Jamie.' Her voice sounded strained. 'That's one of the things I wanted to tell you.' She bit her lip and glanced uncertainly over her shoulder. It had started to snow and Jamie felt cold standing in front of the open door. 'You'd better come in,' she said grudgingly.

'Thanks.' Wanda followed her into the sitting-room, and following Jamie's example sat down.

'I could tell at lunchtime that you weren't pleased to see me.'

'How very astute of you!'

Wanda coloured again.

'Jamie, I know you've no reason to like me, but I felt I had to apologise to you for those lies I told you. Oh, I realise that you and Jake have sorted things out now, and that you obviously know that I lied—I can also see that you haven't told Jake, otherwise I doubt he'd even have spoken to me. I wanted to thank you for that. I suppose you've guessed that I did it because I was frantically jealous of you. I'd fancied myself in love with Jake for months, I'd even managed to convince myself that I was in with a chance, but of course as far as Jake was concerned I was never anything more than a girl he was vaguely friendly with.

'When I saw him with you and realised how he felt about you, it was one of the worst moments of my life. That doesn't excuse what I did, I know.' She spread her hands in a gesture of self-dislike. 'I think I must have gone a little crazy. When I told Gavin he said it sounded more like delayed adolescent madness than anything else. I think I reacted so violently because inwardly I knew I'd never stood a chance with Jake, but I couldn't bear to stand by and see you enjoying the happiness I felt should have been mine. It made no difference that Jake loved you and not me, I managed to convince myself if you weren't there that Jake would turn to me. And fate really seemed to be on my side, of course, when you walked in and caught me kissing Jake. I really threw myself at him that day—a last-ditch attempt to get him interested. I was lucky, he let me down lightly, like the gentleman he is.' She grimaced ruefully. 'God, the arrogance of the young!

When I saw what I'd done to Jake after you left, the truth finally hit me, but I was too much of a coward to tell him the truth, and then I managed to convince myself that if you had really loved him, you'd never have believed my lies.

'I went to America two months after you and Jake split up—that was where I met Gavin. He was involved in some litigation with a company out there. This is the first time I've seen Jake since you left him. I couldn't believe it when he told me the two of you were married. I felt so relieved, but I felt I had to come here and see you to apologise for my jealous lies.

'Jake was telling me today that there's never been anyone else but you for him. He said it was probably just as well you didn't marry six years ago, that he felt on reflection that you were probably too young, and that you might have grown to resent him for tying you down too soon. He was a little embarrassed talking about it—you know how men are, but after all I'd seen the state he was in just after you left. It almost destroyed him.

'Look,' she added awkwardly, 'if you'd rather cancel tonight . . .'

Jamie stared at her as though she didn't know what she was talking about. 'Cancel? Oh no,' she said absently. 'We're both looking forward to it.'

'Then I'm forgiven for what I did?' asked Wanda. 'I've often wanted to get in touch with you, to tell you. More so since I've met Gavin, but I didn't have your address, and to be honest it wasn't easy to face up to what I'd done.' She made a wry face. 'It isn't always possible to admit that one has a far from attractive side to one's nature. I just hope it's one that I have well under control now.' She got up and Jamie followed her to the door.

'Don't worry about it,' she told her quietly. 'And... thanks for coming to see me.'

When she had closed the door Jamie walked slowly back to her chair, sinking down into it and closing her eyes.

Wanda had lied. There had been no mistaking the deep sincerity of what the other woman had told her today. 'Wanda is a friend, nothing more,' Jake had told her, and she had thought him a liar. Jake loved her. Impossible. Impossible that he could have loved her as passionately as Wanda had intimated and done nothing about it. But he had done something, hadn't he? He had married her.

But if he loved her why had he not made at least some effort to tell her, to talk to her?

Because she had never let him, she acknowledged achingly. Since the day she left she had deliberately held him at a distance. Jake in love with her? Loving her with the same intensity of emotion she felt for him? It seemed impossible. She got up, and paced the room as she tried to sort some order into her whirlingly chaotic thoughts.

Why impossible? she asked herself. She had believed once that he loved her. But he had never made any attempt to pursue her, to bring her back.

He thought perhaps he was tying you down too young, Wanda had said. Was that why? But no, if Jake loved her he would be with her now, not skiing alone, apparently quite content to be without her. She paced restlessly, torn between hope and fear, too stunned by Wanda's revelations to know yet what they might or might not mean.

After all Jake wasn't a boy; surely had he wanted to do so he could have found a way to tell her how he felt?

But he had told her once; and she had rejected him, flinging his love back in his face and telling him that she wanted London and a career instead.

The sudden harsh purr of the telephone surprised her. She looked at it without moving and then picked up the receiver unsteadily, tensing in the expectation of hearing Jake's voice.

When instead she heard her mother's, her first re-action was one of shock, hard on the heels of which came dread.

'Mark,' she managed to get out shakily, but the bub-bling happiness with which her fears were dismissed was instantly reassuring.

'I *am* ringing about Mark,' her mother agreed. 'But with good news, not bad. He was due to go and have an-other check just before you got married, but we kept it from you both, not wanting to worry you. The results are through now and the doctors are confident that with the progress he's made and the new drug that's expected to come on to the market later this year he will have an ex-cellent chance of leading a near-to-normal life.'

'Where's Jake?' her mother asked when Jamie had finished expressing her thrilled relief.

'Er——out skiing.' Purposefully she kept her tone vague.

'Is he really? Mark will have lost his bet with him then,' she chuckled. 'He bet him before he left that after wait-ing all these years for you, he wouldn't be able to drag himself away from your side for more than half a dozen minutes at a time. Poor Jake, I'm afraid he's had to endure rather a lot of teasing from Mark over the years because of his feelings for you. I don't know what went wrong between the pair of you all those years ago, and I never asked you because you always made it so obvious that the whole subject was off limits, but I'm so glad you were able to find your way back together again.'

'You knew...you knew about Jake and me before?' Jamie couldn't keep the astonishment out of her voice. 'But how?'

This time her mother's voice was slightly rueful.

'Well, you didn't exactly try to conceal the mammoth crush you had on him, and Jake admitted to us both that he was concerned that because of the way he felt about you he might be tempted into taking advantage of it—of forcing you into a more permanent relationship than you really wanted. When he phoned us to say that you were waiting for us to come back from holiday so that you could get engaged, I must admit that both Mark and I were concerned. You were so very young, with hardly any experience of life at all, but Jake was convinced that you felt as strongly about him as he did about you.

'When we got home and found that you'd gone, we guessed right away, of course, that you'd had second thoughts. Poor Jake, for a while I thought he'd never get over it. Until recently Mark had begun to think that he'd never get married.'

'Until he told you he was bringing his bride-to-be home for Christmas, you mean?' Jamie interrupted.

'Well, no, not then. After all that was a long-standing joke between Jake and your father. He promised to do that every year. It was his way of letting us know that his feelings hadn't changed, I think. No, Mark began to hope that things had changed when Jake telephoned to tell us that he was bringing you home with him for Christmas. You'd made such a point of avoiding him for so long that Mark felt sure you were coming back as something more than stepbrother and sister.'

'Well, he certainly didn't show it,' Jamie murmured.

'Of course he didn't want to embarrass Jake. Don't forget, darling, that for a man as arrogantly masculine as Jake, it's a very difficult thing to admit that you're desperately in love with a woman who doesn't want you, and Jake had made his feelings about you pretty clear to your father and me.

'I think you were barely sixteen when he first told us how he felt about you. We were both very concerned. After all, he was well into his twenties, with quite a wide experience of life, and Mark and I were worried that Jake might be tempted to use his family relationship with you to draw you into a committed relationship before you were mature enough for it. He was very much aware of that temptation himself. He was completely open and honest with us, and I felt very sorry for him when you went away.'

'I thought he was marrying me because Mark's will shared out his assets between us.'

There was a small silence, and then her mother said in a shocked voice,

'Jamie darling, how on earth could you think that? And besides, as I'm sure you know now, Jake inherited a very large sum of money indeed from his mother's family—much more than Mark will be able to leave. Still, it's all over and done with now, I'm glad to say. We're both very pleased with the way it's worked out for you. Quite honestly I think you're both better equipped for marriage now than you were six years ago. You've had the opportunity to experience life for yourself, so that you can meet Jake on equal terms, and losing you has tempered that arrogant side of Jake's nature that can be as infuriating as it is endearing. Whenever Mark particularly annoys me by being traditionally chauvinistic, I try to remind myself that the reverse side of the same coin is that he is also a very protective and tender man who would never dream of putting his own desires before those of his wife and family. No one can alter their temperament completely, only temper it, and Jake is very much his father's son, brought up to believe that it is his duty and responsibility to protect the women in his life, although I think that Jake has come to realise now that women too need some independence.'

They chatted on for a few more minutes, her mother relating to Jamie the guests' enjoyment of the wedding, and when she hung up the sky was already starting to darken.

Very thoughtfully Jamie stared out into the gathering gloom. It had to be true. Her mother wouldn't lie to her; and she could see no reason at all for Jake to have lied to their parents, and certainly not over such a long period of time.

He loved her. She tasted the words, letting them roll round in her mind, absorbing the implications that went with them, feeling something expand and blossom into wild and glorious life.

The phone rang again. She picked it up automatically. 'Jamie, it's Wanda. I'm afraid I'm going to have to cancel tonight, after all. Gavin has got caught up in Innsbruck and I'm going to spend the night there with him. I hope, though, we should be able to get together before you leave.'

Strangely she felt no resentment towards Wanda, Jamie discovered as she replaced the receiver; there was no room for that, really. She was dizzy, almost drunk in fact, on the delirious joy that had obliterated everything else. Jake loved her. Suddenly her whole life had been transformed, and if she looked carefully enough couldn't she see the seeds of jealousy in comments she had previously thought were prompted by sarcasm? Before, the possibility of Jake caring about her had been so remote that she had seen his attitude towards her as being prompted by malice and cruelty; now she realised that like her he had been adopting a protective disguise.

What would he say when he...? Abruptly she frowned, suddenly brought face to face with the impossibility of simply blurting out that she had discovered how he felt about her. He was bound to deny it—that's what she would have done in the same circumstances. He might not even be inclined to believe her if she told him she loved him. They were married, but as far as he was concerned it was a marriage he had forced on her—a fact of which she had not stopped reminding him since the day he announced their engagement.

Absently gnawing her lip, she was wondering what on earth she was going to do when the door opened and Jake walked in.

'Sorry to be so late,' he said tersely, 'I got chatting with one of the ski-instructors. He was telling me about a new cross-country ski-trail they've just opened. It's a full-day affair, and they're trying to make up the numbers for a party large enough to make it worth the guide's while.'

'I suppose it would be too difficult for me?' Jamie asked him eagerly, forgetting how they had parted. She ached to go to him and hold him in her arms, to beg him to forgive her for the past, but she was brought abruptly out of this daydream by the look on his face.

'Rather overdoing it, aren't you?' he mocked. 'There's no need to play the eager wife for *my* benefit, Jamie. I already know how you feel—God knows you've made it plain enough. I'd better go upstairs and shower if we're going out for dinner.'

'It's off,' Jamie told him absently. 'Wanda rang; her husband's stuck in Innsbruck and she's gone down there to be with him. She said she'd make a fresh date when they get back. Quite a coincidence you running into her here after all this time.'

He gave her a sharp look as though suspecting her of sarcasm, and when he saw nothing in her face agreed casually, 'I suppose it is. She and I came here as part of a party about six years ago. They'd only just built the hotel then. I haven't seen her here since.'

'No, she said it was only her husband's business that brought them here now. Apparently most of his work is connected with companies in the States.'

'When did she tell you that?'

He looked sharply at her, and Jamie felt her face sting with colour. 'She came to see me earlier this afternoon. We had quite a long chat.'

Perhaps this was her chance. She held her breath, mentally willing him to ask what they had talked about, but instead he simply shrugged and headed for the stairs, throwing over his shoulder, 'Okay if I use the bathroom first?'

Dispirited, Jamie nodded her head.

Jake was already in the shower when the telephone rang and the girl on the reception desk asked Jamie if they planned to eat at the hotel that evening or if they wanted to order a meal at the chalet.

Thinking quickly, Jamie decided she would have far more chance of talking to Jake intimately if they were alone, and then she remembered that the freezer was stuffed full of ready-prepared food. It would be quite simple for her to conjure up a meal for them both.

Refusing both offers, she thanked the girl and then hung up.

It was only when Jake was making love to her that he revealed anything of his feelings; with hindsight she recognised that now. Slowly a plan began to take shape in her mind. She wandered into the kitchen and examined the contents of the freezer. Just as she thought; they were hardly likely to starve.

She was just walking back into the sitting-room when she heard the bathroom door open. When she called to him, Jake came to stand at the top of the stairs. His hair was damp and clung sleekly to his skull, his towelling robe open at the throat. Tiny beads of moisture clung to his skin, and Jamie felt her insides melt. For all these years she had fought to suppress her desire for him, and now it welled up inside her with a force she need no longer deny. The urge to touch him was so strong that she had to look away.

'Er...I thought we could eat here tonight. I'm...I'm a little bit tired.' She saw that he was frowning, and ridiculously crossed her fingers behind her back.

'If that's what you want.' His voice was terse. He turned away and walked into their bedroom.

Jamie followed him upstairs and pushed open the bedroom door. He looked at her in surprise, his eyebrows lifting.

'I thought I might as well have a shower and get changed myself,' she told him lightly, walking past him to find clean underwear, and picking up her robe.

'I wouldn't mind a drink, if you could pour me one,' she added, opening the door and praying that he wouldn't question why she hadn't brought a drink upstairs with her if she wanted one, but to her relief he merely commented, 'I shouldn't think the bar runs to anything over-exotic. What did you have in mind?'

'Oh, a gin and tonic, please.'

He was still in the bedroom when she walked through into the bathroom, the sharp scent of his cologne hanging faintly on the air.

Looking thoughtfully at the jacuzzi, Jamie walked over to it, and studied the instructions taped to the side. It sounded easy enough.

Putting her plan into action was easy enough when she had something physical to do, but when she stepped back to watch the whirlpool bath quickly filling, all sorts of doubts attacked her. What if her plan failed? What if after all Jake didn't love her, what if...

What if you mess up the rest of your life because you lose your courage? she asked herself wryly. Wasn't there a saying about the longest journey beginning with the first step? Well, if she didn't take that first step she might lose the chance to begin the journey that could, if she was lucky, lead to the discovery that Jake loved her as much as she loved him.

Firmly dismissing her doubts, she set the whirlpool effect in motion. Heavens, it looked and sounded like a witch's cauldron! She watched fascinated for several seconds until the sound of Jake going downstairs reminded her of what she should be doing.

Stepping out of her clothes, she pinned her hair up on top of her head, and stepped towards the pool. The lighting in the bathroom was overhead and quite harsh, but in the area around the pool she noticed it was much more subdued and further muted by the banking of green plants which screened it from the more functional part of the room. She switched off the main lights, grinning a little to herself at the much softer glow that was left.

The pool had seating round its octagonal sides, and she positioned herself on one of them so that she was facing the door. As she heard Jake come up the stairs her tension increased, butterflies swarming frantically in her stomach.

He opened the door and said curtly, 'Here's your drink. Where...?'

Jamie had very rarely seen Jake discomposed, but he was now. For several seconds he simply stood and stared at her.

'Oh, you've brought my drink. Good. Could you bring it over here for me, please, Jake?'

She hoped he wouldn't even begin to guess how nervous she felt. As he walked towards her she sat up a little, knowing that in doing so she was revealing the upper curves of her breasts.

He reached her and put the glass into the hand she stretched out. Her nerves as taut as fine-drawn wire, Jamie took a deep breath to steady herself and then said serenely, 'I thought I might as well try the jacuzzi as it was here.' She looked up at him below her lashes and saw that he was studying her with intense concentration.

'It's really rather nice,' she added demurely. 'Why don't you join me?'

Her legs floated horizontally under the gentle buffet of the water jets, and she deliberately looked lazily at her toes. If he rejected her now, she had no idea what on earth she was going to do. She had never in her life made a sexual advance to any man, and to be doing so now to her own husband felt so bizarre that half of her couldn't actually believe what she was doing.

Jake was completely silent, and sipping her drink she risked a nervous glance at him.

His chest rose and fell sharply as though he was having trouble regulating his breathing, a dark tide of colour surging up under his skin. His fingers caught her wrist and tightened round it, and for one appalled moment Jamie thought he was going to pull her out. Instead he said unsteadily,

'Are you sure you know what you're doing?'

Her tension started to ease. 'Very sure,' she told him softly, making herself meet his eyes.

Without taking his eyes off her he stripped off his clothes and slid into the water on the opposite side of the spa.

'Come here,' he said thickly.

Letting instinct and emotion guide her, Jamie went eagerly to him, kneeling down in front of him, her hands on his knees, the water lapping at her shoulders.

'Jamie.' His eyes were shadowed, faintly sombre, and not wanting him to start questioning her behaviour Jamie begged impulsively, 'Kiss me, Jake.'

She leaned forwards, sliding her arms round his neck, moving closer to him so that his thighs touched her skin and her breasts pressed gently against his chest. Without giving him time to move, she pressed her mouth to his throat, biting it gently.

'Jamie.'

She heard the wonder in his voice and felt the bemusement in his touch as his fingers curled against her skin, urging her lips to move along the strong column of his throat.

She kissed him gently, exploring the shape of his ear, the firm line of his jaw, her tongue making teasingly light forays against his mouth.

She heard him groan and felt the shudder that surged through him as he tried to hold her in his arms, but she wriggled away, laughing softly, letting her hands glide slowly over him. He shuddered again, a hectic flush darkening his skin, his body fully aroused as he caught hold of her and pulled her against his body.

'Jamie.' His voice was thick and unsteady. 'For God's sake, what...?'

She moved slowly against him, rubbing her body sinuously against his, glorying in his harshly indrawn gasp of arousal, felinely proud of the voluptuous effect of her touch.

'Take me to bed, Jake,' she murmured against his mouth. She started to climb out of the jacuzzi, stifling her own inner doubts and tension as Jake stood up and lifted her in his arms.

Both of them were damp, but it didn't seem to matter, and besides, there were things she wanted to do to Jake; ways she wanted to love him that made her impatient of even the briefest delay.

She had taken the initiative and she was determined to keep it at least until she had managed to weaken Jake's resistance to the point where she might be able to get him to listen to her.

As he lowered her on to the bed, she reached up and kissed him, running her tongue softly against his mouth, stroking her fingers over his skin.

'Jamie.'

His hand cupped her breast, his hoarse cry of need stifled by the hot demand of his mouth on her own. Beneath her fingertips his skin burned, her purpose forgotten whilst she gave herself up to the fierceness of his kiss.

All of her felt deliciously yielding and weak; but she mustn't let desire overwhelm her—not yet.

When his mouth released hers, she pushed him gently back against the bed, placing her lips against his chest, and then lazily letting her mouth trace a sensual path down his body.

When he realised what she intended to do, at first he tried to resist her, reaching down to lock his fingers round her wrists and pull her away. But she bit gently into the firm flesh of his thigh, and let her tongue draw teasing circles of fire against his skin until he was unable to withstand the pleasure, and was forced, as she had been with him, to abandon himself to his own desire and the loving intimacy of her hands and mouth.

As hers had done, his body arched in blind supplication, wanting what his brain was struggling not to permit.

What she had started as a means of showing him her love had aroused her as much as it had aroused him, and when he took hold of her, rolling her underneath him, burying himself in the moist heat of her, Jamie moaned in frantic pleasure, wrapping herself round him, meeting the aching need of his kiss.

Their climax was mutually explosive, a physical expression of the harmony their minds had yet to know, Jamie thought dizzily as she drifted back from the heights of pleasure. She was lying on her side, her arms wrapped round Jake. Beneath her cheek she could feel the fierce thud of his heart, his breathing still harsh in her ear.

Contentedly she touched his chest, teasing her fingers through the fine dark hair, and laughing softly when he groaned,

'My God, you've exhausted me Jamie! What happened?'

'You mean you don't know?' She opened her eyes wide and lifted her head to peer down into his face.

The mockery in his eyes was replaced by a look of intense scrutiny. 'Dare I ask you what all that was about?' he said quietly.

She didn't pretend not to understand. This was after all what she had wanted—the intimacy and warmth of his arms; his body and mind relaxed and sated by love; his guard down, so that she could at least try to reach him.

'Oh, it's just my way of trying to show you how much I love you.'

As she had known he would, he tensed up, his arms moving to push her away, his eyes cold and angry as he glared at her.

'I don't know what you think you're playing at, Jamie,' he began bitterly.

'Why should I be playing?'

'Why?' He was breathing harshly, his eyes glittering with anger. 'You can actually ask me *that*? Six years ago you told me you loved me, and then you walked out on me claiming that you'd decided you wanted a career instead. Since then you've avoided me like the plague. Even today. . .'

'I lied to you, Jake.' The enormity of the admission nearly destroyed her courage. She couldn't look at him. 'I've always loved you, but . . . I ran away because I thought you didn't love me, that you were marrying me because—well, because of your father's will.'

'You what?'

He sat up, pulling her to her knees, almost shaking her as he roared the words. 'You thought...? What the hell gave you a crazy idea like that?'

'Who,' she corrected him lightly. 'Who, Jake, and it was Wanda.'

Falteringly she told him what the other woman had said, and how she had learned the truth.

'Why on earth didn't you say something to me? Why was it easier to believe Wanda than to believe me—the man you supposedly loved?'

'Jake, I was eighteen, and a very naïve eighteen at that. I suppose part of me never really believed that you did love me, that this magnificent being whom I'd practically worshipped could actually want me as much as I wanted him.'

She watched the anger die from his eyes and his face lose some of its colour.

'I ought to wring your bloody neck,' he said thickly. 'When I think of what you've put us both through, to say nothing of the years we've lost. I ought to,' he groaned, 'but right now all I can think of doing is this.'

This was the fierce pressure of his mouth on her own, demanding that she give way to his male dominance.

When he finally drew his mouth away, his voice was raw with a mingling of pain and self-mockery.

'I've been waiting years for you to change your mind, to grow tired of London and your career. I dared not go after you at first, I was too scared that I might panic you into running even further. I've carried my feelings for you around with me like a sick obsession for six years, telling myself I ought to find myself someone else, knowing it was impossible, unable even physically to make love to another woman. I've torn myself apart over the way I've felt about you, and now you tell me it was all unnecessary, all caused by someone else's lies.'

Knowing what he was feeling Jamie said gently,

'Jake perhaps it *was* all for the best. I was very naïve and immature at eighteen; then I could never have met you as an equal, and I'm pretty sure you would soon have outgrown me.'

'Are you trying to convince me that Wanda did us a favour?' he demanded.

'What about Amanda?' Jamie reminded him wryly. 'You seemed pretty determined to marry her.'

'*You* were the one who jumped to that conclusion initially, I just played along with it to make you jealous.'

'But Amanda herself. . .'

Jake grinned. 'Her father was coming on pretty heavily to me, hinting that he wanted me as a son-in-law, and I decided the easiest and least painful way of putting a stop to that was to terrify Amanda into convincing her father that I was the last person she wanted as a husband. What I didn't bargain for was that she would run straight to you for help, or that you would actually believe I wanted any woman in my life but you,' he added huskily.

He bent his head towards her, but Jamie pushed him away firmly. 'That doesn't explain the way you tricked me into marriage,' she reminded him.

'Oh, that.' Again he grinned. 'You were the one who decided I was going to marry Amanda. I just carried it a step further, and decided that since you were so determined to marry me off, I might as well have the bride of my choice. I must admit I was a little surprised at how easy it was to persuade you to go along with it. I thought I'd discovered the reason for that last night,' he added grimly, adding when she frowned, 'Your sexual response to me and the fact that you said there'd been no one else. I thought you were just using me for physical release.'

Jamie shook her head. 'You frightened me, made me feel vulnerable. How could I want you like that? Love you so much when you didn't love me?'

'Not love you?' Jake groaned. 'Every time I touched you I betrayed how I feel about you. You had to be blind not to see it. I'm thirty-two years old, and you're the only woman who can send me up in flames like that.

'I don't expect you to give up everything you've worked for, you know, Jamie,' he said abruptly. 'You've built up a career for yourself and . . .'

She shook her head, quickly interrupting him. 'Ralph will be more than happy to buy me out. I shall be quite content with a much more modest sort of operation—the kind that can adapt easily to the pressure of family life,' she added with a grin. 'Lots of family life. Heavens!' She suddenly remembered that she hadn't told him about his father, adding that it was her conversation with her mother that had convinced her that Wanda had been right when she said he loved her.

'It's frightening to contemplate the fragile thread of coincidence on which our happiness hangs,' he murmured soberly, adding with a faint grimace, 'Mind you, if you'd carried on being as responsive to me as you were last night, I doubt I could have held out long without telling you how I felt. I only just managed to stop myself last night because I was terrified of frightening you away. There's only one thing that still worries me.'

'Oh?'

'Mmm. Where, I wonder, did you learn to become such an accomplished seductress?'

Jamie laughed. 'Ah, well,' she teased. 'It was like this. I've always learned best by example, and I have this husband . . .' She bent her head and whispered provocatively in his ear until he took her in his arms and murmured dulcetly,

'Well, in that case . . .'

It was much, much later when Jamie suddenly remembered they had had nothing to eat, and as they padded companionably around the kitchen preparing themselves a meal, she reflected that although the homely task was far from romantic, she was happier now than at any other time in her life.

Jake stopped cutting the bread for their scrambled eggs and smiled at her.

'What are you thinking?' she asked him dreamily, anticipating his loving response.

Instead he grinned wickedly and teased, 'I'm just wondering what our children will say when I tell them their mother seduced me in a jacuzzi.'

'You dare tell anyone that!' Jamie threatened scarlet-faced, her indignation forgotten as Jake took her in his arms and whispered softly,

'I won't. Just as long as you promise me you'll do it again—soon.'

Harlequin Presents

Coming Next Month

Available in January wherever paperback books are sold, or through Harlequin Reader Service:

In the U.S.
901 Fuhrmann Blvd.
P.O. Box 1397
Buffalo, N.Y. 14240-1397

In Canada
P.O. Box 603
Fort Erie, Ontario
L2A 5X3

Take 4 books
& a surprise gift
FREE

SPECIAL LIMITED-TIME OFFER

Mail to   **Harlequin Reader Service**®

In the U.S.   In Canada
901 Fuhrmann Blvd.   P.O. Box 609
P.O. Box 1394   Fort Erie, Ontario
Buffalo, N.Y. 14240-1394   L2A 5X3

YES!   Please send me 4 free Harlequin Romance® novels and my free surprise gift. Then send me 8 brand-new novels every month as they come off the presses. Bill me at the low price of $1.99 each*—an 11% saving off the retail price. There are no shipping, handling or other hidden costs. There is no minimum number of books I must purchase. I can always return a shipment and cancel at any time. Even if I never buy another book from Harlequin, the 4 free novels and the surprise gift are mine to keep forever.   118 BPR BP7F

*Plus 89¢ postage and handling per shipment in Canada.

Name	(PLEASE PRINT)	
Address		Apt. No.
City	State/Prov.	Zip/Postal Code

This offer is limited to one order per household and not valid to present subscribers. Price is subject to change.   DOR-SUB-1D

ATTRACTIVE, SPACE SAVING BOOK RACK

Display your most prized novels on this handsome and sturdy book rack. The hand-rubbed walnut finish will blend into your library decor with quiet elegance, providing a practical organizer for your favorite hard-or soft-covered books.

Only $9.95

Approximately 16" x 8" when assembled

Assembles in seconds!

To order, rush your name, address and zip code, along with a check or money order for $10.70* ($9.95 plus 75¢ postage and handling) payable to *Harlequin Reader Service*:

Harlequin Reader Service
Book Rack Offer
901 Fuhrmann Blvd.
P.O. Box 1396
Buffalo, NY 14269-1396

Offer not available in Canada.

BKR-1A

*New York and Iowa residents add appropriate sales tax.

*Coming Soon
from Harlequin...*

GIFTS FROM THE HEART

**Watch for it
in February**